"What are you doing?"

Chandler poured himself a mug of coffee. "What do you mean?"

Henry knew exactly what he was doing. He was trying to take over her renovation project.

"What are you doing with the cabinets?" she demanded.

He leaned casually against the sink. "*Mam* told me she's wanted to renovate her kitchen for years. I'm a carpenter. I build cabinets and install them, so I will put them in for her."

"*Ya*, Edee does want her kitchen renovated. Which is why *I'm* doing it," she blurted.

The moment the words were out of her mouth, she wished she could take them back. What if Edee had changed her mind and asked her son to do it. Henry would be devastated if she lost the job. She'd worked months planning the project.

She took a step toward Chandler, trying to remain calm. "Your mother hired me," she said firmly. "I'll be doing the work."

"You're a *contractor*?"

He didn't have to say what he meant. He was questioning the idea that a *woman* could do the work.

Emma Miller lives quietly in her old farmhouse in rural Delaware. Fortunate enough to have been born into a family of strong faith, she grew up on a dairy farm, surrounded by loving parents, siblings, grandparents, aunts, uncles and cousins. Emma was educated in local schools and once taught in an Amish schoolhouse. When she's not caring for her large family, reading and writing are her favorite pastimes.

Books by Emma Miller

Love Inspired

Seven Amish Sisters

Visit the Author Profile page at LoveInspired.com for more titles.

An Unconventional Amish Pair

EMMA MILLER

LOVE INSPIRED
INSPIRATIONAL ROMANCE

LOVE INSPIRED®

INSPIRATIONAL ROMANCE

Recycling programs for this product may not exist in your area.

ISBN-13: 978-1-335-59870-7

An Unconventional Amish Pair

Copyright © 2024 by Emma Miller

Love Inspired
22 Adelaide St. West, 41st Floor
Toronto, Ontario M5H 4E3, Canada
www.LoveInspired.com

Printed in U.S.A.

And he said unto him, Son, thou art ever with me, and all that I have is thine.
—*Luke* 15:31

Chapter One

Spring,
Kent County, Delaware

Henrietta Koffman held tightly to the aluminum ladder with both hands and squeezed her eyes shut. Counting to three, she breathed deeply to calm her pounding heart. The good Lord took His faithful in His own time, but this was not how she wanted to go. This was not how she wanted her family to remember her—falling to her death off a roof. Especially when no one thought she should have taken this job for Edee Gingerich in the first place.

"Please, *Gott*," she whispered. "Not today. I promise I'll try to do better. I'll be more devout. No more naps during Sunday service, even if the sermon goes on too long."

The previous night, this had seemed like such a good idea. Even though she wasn't fond of heights, she wanted to be sure the chimney cap hadn't been knocked off when she removed the stovepipe below. All she had to do was climb the ladder two stories up, attach an eyebolt to the roof and hook the harness she'd borrowed from her brother-in-law to the eyebolt. Then she would walk across the roof to the ridge and follow it to the chimney.

It was just a matter of getting *to* the chimney now, but she felt as if her feet were glued to the rung of the ladder. One more step and she would be on the roof. The anchor plate was already attached, the harness clipped in. If she fell, she'd only drop a few feet before the harness caught on its tether, and she'd be all right. Her brother-in-law Jack, a building contractor, promised she'd be fine, joking that he'd fallen several times over the years and never had any injury but a bruised ego when his employees had seen him slip. He had offered to go up on Edee Gingerich's roof for her, but Henry refused his help. This was her job; she'd written up the estimate, then the contract, and secured the kitchen renovation project completely on her own, and she would do the work herself. She intended to prove to those who thought she couldn't do it that they were wrong.

Standing thirty feet in the air on a ladder, the spring breeze tugging at her hair covered in a scarf, she was having second thoughts. Her eyes closed; she pretended her feet were on the ground. She listened to the birdsong in the blossoming trees surrounding the house and inhaled the sweet scent of freshly turned soil in the neighboring fields.

Would it have been so terrible for her to let Jack do this one little thing for her? But that was a moot point now because here she was, standing on the ladder.

"I'm not a quitter," she mumbled, forcing herself to open her eyes again. From her perch, she watched an older model white pickup slowly drive by the house. Then, taking a deep breath, she stepped onto the asphalt-shingled roof. However, she miscalculated: her foot caught on the edge of the rain gutter, and she fell onto the roof with a loud exhalation of air.

"Ouch," she muttered as the metal clips of the harness cut into her.

Thank goodness Edee had stayed in the house. She couldn't imagine what she looked like lying on the roof in her father's work pants and shirt. Her uncle, the bishop of her church district, would have a fit if he knew his niece was wearing men's clothes. But wearing a dress and prayer *kapp* didn't make sense while doing construction work; it was uncomfortable, limiting and could even be dangerous. So she'd left her family's house that morning wearing a blue dress and changed after she arrived. She'd put her dress back on before her boyfriend, Sam, picked her up, and no one would be the wiser but Edee—and the widow would never tell.

Boyfriend? she thought. It was the first time she'd put his name and that word together. Was the bushy-browed Sam her boyfriend? There had been no conversation between them about walking out together, although they saw each other every weekend attending one community event or another. And now, he would pick her up most days from Edee's because he worked for Jack's construction company and was the foreman for a job they were doing in Rose Valley, where Edee lived.

The reminder that Sam would come for her within the hour motivated her to roll over and sit up. The view through the old oak trees was beautiful from the rooftop. She studied the county road in front of the house as the same white pickup passed again going in the opposite direction. Across the way, Edee's neighbor walked behind a plow pulled by two Percheron horses, turning over the spring soil for planting. She raised her face to the sun's warmth and felt the slight breeze on her cheeks. Saying a quick prayer for her safety, she gritted her teeth and rolled onto her side to come to her feet.

It took two tries to stand because it was

windier than she'd anticipated. But she managed to get to a crouching position and then slowly stood. Finding her balance, she watched the white pickup go by the house yet again. It was probably someone looking for fresh eggs for sale. Edee's road was mostly Amish farms; *Englishers* were always driving up and down, looking for eggs, firewood or fresh produce for sale. Moving carefully, she turned to face the roof's ridge and eyed the chimney. She would need to sink another anchor point into the roof and attach the harness higher. Jack said that would keep her from falling too far if she slipped from the top.

"Just a short walk," she said aloud as she checked to be sure the harness was still secure across her chest. "Fifteen feet. Maybe twenty. Easy peasy."

She ignored her fluttering heart and took one step, then another, and wobbled. The wind had picked up, and the branches of the live oak tree in the backyard swayed. The roof's incline was more severe than it had seemed from the ground. She put out her hands for balance and took another step, feeling the tug of the rope clipped to the harness. She wondered if she'd be able to walk easier without it and considered unhooking herself, but then thought better of it.

She had promised Jack she would use the harness and was a woman of her word.

She fixed her gaze on the chimney. "Easy peasy," she repeated, gritting her teeth.

Henry didn't know what happened next. One moment she was walking toward the chimney, and the next she was falling forward. She cried out as she went down. She was able to put out her hands to break her fall, but she felt a rough shingle scrape her cheek. Just as she thought she was safe, she began to slide down the sloped roof.

"No, no, no," she cried, clawing with her hands, trying to slow her descent. But there was nothing to grab onto. Her feet hit the ladder hard, and she felt it give way. She heard it clatter to the ground just as she slipped over the roof's edge, hands and feet flailing wildly. The rope from the harness caught her so hard that it knocked the wind out of her, and for a few seconds she dangled off the roof, swaying, her eyes squeezed shut. But slowly her body came to rest at the end of the rope.

Her eyes flew open, and against her will, her gaze fell to the grass two stories below, where the ladder lay. *Guess I should have asked Jack what to do if I did fall*, she thought.

Now what? The harness was so tight around her that she couldn't fully inhale, and she was starting to feel the tightness of panic in her chest. Her heart beat fast, and she breathed in short gasps. How was she going to get help? Even if she shouted, Edee would never hear her from inside.

"You all right?" a male voice called from below.

Startled, Henry looked down to see an *Englisher* in blue jeans, a flannel shirt and a baseball cap. He was twenty-five maybe, with butter-yellow blond hair that fell over one eye, and a dimple on his square chin. "Um...*ya*," she said, her cheeks hot with embarrassment. No, she was beyond embarrassment; she was mortified to be hanging from a roof dressed in her father's clothes. "*Ya*, yes, I'm okay. Not hurt." *Where did he come from?* she wondered. Then she saw a white pickup parked in the lane. It was the same one she'd noticed minutes ago.

He gazed up at her, shading his eyes from the sun with his hand. "If I can get the ladder right next to you, can you climb down? I'll hold it for you. Or I can come up to help you."

"No need to come up," she assured him, sounding calmer than she felt. "If you could get the ladder back up, I can manage." All she could think of now was getting off this roof before Sam showed up. If she didn't, he'd tell everyone in Honeycomb what had happened, and her uncle would be paying a call to discuss giving up her silly notion of working for women like Edee who couldn't afford the big companies or didn't want male strangers in their homes. Poor Edee's eldest son died three years ago, and her younger son left the church eight years ago and was never seen again.

"Just put the ladder back up, please," she said, her voice squeaking. Thank goodness this handsome man was a stranger and she would never have to see him again.

"You sure you're okay?" he asked again.

"I'm fine," she insisted. "Just put the ladder back up! Please," she added, softening her tone.

"No worries." He smiled up at her, seeming to take no offense. "You'll be down in a jiffy."

And she was.

He stood the ladder up and held it until she was standing on firm ground again. "Thank you," she said as she freed herself from the harness. Now that she was safe, she felt flustered. She didn't like feeling so vulnerable and, even more, disliked the thought that a stranger saw her this way.

"You're welcome." He hooked his thumbs into the pockets of his Levi's jeans and smiled.

He was good-looking, and he knew it. He wasn't the kind of man Henry ordinarily was drawn to. The handsome ones who knew they were handsome were usually self-centered and useless, in her opinion. But she felt herself blush as he studied her. He hadn't said anything about her unusual attire, but then she wondered if he even realized she was Amish.

"Can I ask what you were doing up there?"

"I wanted to check to be sure the chimney cap was properly reseated," Henry explained. "This morning, we pulled the stovepipe down inside, and I was worried the cap had been jostled."

He gazed up at the roof. "Want me to go up and check? It would only take me a minute. Honestly, I'm not crazy about heights, but I'd do it for you." Again the charming smile.

"No, thank you." She threw the harness over her shoulder. "I'll take care of it tomorrow," she said, expecting an argument.

He shrugged. "Okay."

She met his gaze, surprised by his response. Instead of insisting he would do it for her or saying something about how she shouldn't be on the roof, he'd let it drop. It was as if he thought she could do it. This wasn't a response she was used to in her Amish community, especially from a man. Even Sam Yoder, whom she was sort of dating, was always commenting about what he thought women should and shouldn't do, and it was clear he didn't approve of her work. It was too bad this good Samaritan was *English*. Because a man like him would be the kind of man she'd like to marry someday.

"So…" He furrowed his brow as he followed her toward the back porch. "Does…um…does Edee Gingerich still live here?"

She looked at him, surprised to hear him speak the widow's name. Why was he asking? she wondered suspiciously. Had he been casing her house? Was that why he'd driven by several times? A few weeks ago, an Amish widow in another community in Kent County had been robbed. The police later discovered the thieves had been watching her house for days before finally breaking in while the woman was at church.

"Well, thank you again for your help." She offered a quick smile and made a beeline for the back porch, thinking she would go straight in and warn Edee of the suspicious man. Maybe she should consider staying the night with her friend to be sure she was safe.

"So does she live here or not?" he asked, hooking his thumb toward the county road. "Gingerich is on the mailbox."

Henry looked over her shoulder at him, uncomfortable that he was pressing her for the widow's name. "Why do you need to know?" she asked sharply.

Before he could respond, the back door flew open, and Edee appeared. "Chandler!" she cried, rushing across the porch.

Staring at Edee and then the man, Henry stepped out of the widow's way.

"My *sohn*! My *sohn*, you've come home," Edee sobbed.

Henry watched as her friend threw open her arms to embrace the stranger.

This handsome blond was *her son*? This was Chandler, who had left the church and his family years ago? Henry couldn't stop staring as mother and son embraced.

"I prayed you'd come back to me," Edee said, laughing and crying at the same time as she hugged him tightly. "I prayed and prayed because I knew *Gott* would answer my prayers someday."

"Mam," Chandler murmured, wrapping his muscular arms around her small frame and kissing her cheek.

"This is my *sohn*! My Chandler," Edee told Henry. She took his hand and led him across the porch, unashamed of her tears. "Come in, come in. Are you hungry, Chandler? You must be hungry."

Henry stood for a moment in disbelief as she watched them walk into the house. Then, not knowing what else to do, she followed them.

Inside, Henry stood in the doorway between the mudroom and kitchen, watching them as Edee insisted her son sit and began pulling leftovers out of the refrigerator.

"I want to hear everything about you," Edee gushed. "I want to know everywhere you've been. What you've been doing." Beaming, she looked over her shoulder at him as she set containers on the counter. "I want to know all there is to know. But first, you must eat. Did you bring a suitcase? You're staying a bit, aren't you? Please tell me you're staying."

The clock on the wall caught Henry's eye, and she realized Sam would be there momentarily to pick her up. She hadn't loved the idea of giving up the freedom of coming and going to Edee's as she pleased, but she'd accepted the offer after pressure from her family.

Henry eyed Chandler as Edee chattered. Why was he here after all these years? What did he want from his mother? Why would a young man leave his widowed mother in the middle of the night, not contact her to let her know he was alive for eight years and then show up? Was it money he wanted? Was it even safe for her to leave Edee alone with him? "Need any help, Edee?" she asked.

The petite woman in a pale green dress, black stockings and a white apron and prayer *kapp* shook her head. "Indeed not, but you should join us for an early supper. Talk with my Chandler. I know you'll like him. He's a very nice boy. Very kind."

Henry glanced at the clock again. If she didn't hurry, Sam would come up the lane for her, and for some reason she didn't want him to. Why, she wasn't sure. Maybe because she was embarrassed to have felt a momentary attraction to Edee's *English* son and was afraid Sam would somehow know? "*Danki,* but I can't," she told Edee. "Time to go home." Looking once more in the handsome man's direction, she excused herself and went down the hall to change out of her work clothes.

By the time Henry returned to the kitchen dressed as she had left her family home that morning, the widow was busy heating up the leftovers. "I'll see you tomorrow, Edee?"

"*Ya,*" Edee said over her shoulder. "See you tomorrow."

Henry hesitated, glancing in Chandler's direction. "Thank you again for your help." She didn't smile.

He turned in his chair to face her, looking her up and down in surprise. "You're *Amish*?"

She ran her hand over the prayer *kapp* that had replaced the scarf she wore during her workday. "*Ya,* I am."

He grinned at her. "I'd have never guessed."

"A lot of surprising things about this young lady," Edee said, shaking a wooden spoon in Henry's direction.

"And what's this young lady's name?" he asked.

"Henrietta," Henry answered, unsure why she had spoken her given name.

"But we call her Henry," Edee said. "Everyone does. Wait until you get to know her, *sohn.* You're going to love her as much as I do."

"Am I?" His blue eyes, pale like the color of the sky, twinkled as he met Henry's gaze. He was still smiling at her, a brash smile that made her feel off-balance. "I look forward to that," he said, directing his comment to Henry rather than his mother.

Then he winked at Henry, which shocked her so much she rushed out of the house.

Chandler watched the young Amish woman go, then rose from his chair to help his mother. He removed two plates from the cupboard. They were the same plates he fondly remembered using as a child. "Henrietta who?" he asked. "She's not from around here, is she?" He was shocked that Henrietta was Amish, though he hoped it hadn't been too evident. She'd been dressed in work pants and a shirt...on a roof.

How could he have guessed? She wasn't like any Amish woman he'd ever known when he lived here.

"Koffman. Comes from a nice family over in Honeycomb. One of seven sisters. I'm sure you met them at some point. They lost their mother a few years ago and now care for their ailing father. Hard workers, those girls, and as faithful as they come." She eyed her son. "Be the kind of woman a man like you would do well to marry."

He laughed, carrying the plates to the table. "Something tells me that a nice girl like Henrietta isn't looking for a man like me. I was never baptized, remember? And I've been living a sinful life full of motor vehicles and reruns of television sitcoms." He did not mention the cigarettes, beer or any other more shocking things he'd seen or done; he wouldn't do that to his *mam*. But she wasn't a fool. She knew, but there was no reason to speak of it and upset her.

"There's always salvation for a man willing to seek it," she answered firmly as she stirred the leftover succotash she was reheating on the stove. "I've prayed for that, too. Not just for you to come home, but to find your way home to the church."

He couldn't resist a smile. He'd missed his mother so much. She hadn't changed a bit. She always saw the best in people and believed they were fundamentally good. She trusted in God's forgiveness and the salvation He offered. She even believed her wayward son could be saved. He liked to think that was true, but he wasn't sure he believed it.

The eight years he'd been gone had been hard. Lonely. He'd not given up on God, but it had seemed like maybe God had given up on him. When he left Delaware, he had high hopes of finding happiness and fulfillment in the *English* world. He'd thought that walking away from the strict rules he'd been raised with would help him find himself and his place in the world. He'd been wrong.

He'd struggled to find work and never lived in a place half as nice as the home he was standing in now. And even though he'd lived in several states, he'd not found a place he belonged. No matter how he tried, he had never quite fit in with the *English* men his age he worked with. Even though he had been living in the *English* world, it seemed like his heart had never adjusted. Standing here in his boyhood kitchen, it was hard to remember why at eighteen he had so desperately wanted to leave Rose Valley, leave his family and friends.

Chandler regretted now that he hadn't returned sooner. Or at least sent letters occasionally to let his mother know he was okay. For the last year or two, he'd played around with the idea of coming home, but only when he'd learned last week of his brother Joe's death through a friend of a friend had he decided to quit his job in Illinois and return to Delaware. It had broken his heart to know that Joe had been gone two years and here he had been thinking all this time that his big brother was here caring for their mother.

He was relieved to find that she was still on their farm and seemed to be doing well, considering all she'd been through. The barnyard looked well maintained, the exterior of the house had a fresh coat of paint and, from the appearance of the kitchen, she was having some renovations done.

But how did Henrietta, an Amish woman who wore pants and climbed roofs, fit into the picture?

Chapter Two

Just as Henry reached the end of Edee's lane, she spotted Sam approaching. She recognized his small buggy at once, although it looked like every other black buggy in Kent County, Delaware. It was his driving horse that couldn't be missed. Sam had saved money working as a bricklayer for years to buy a buggy and a horse to pull it, and the dapple-gray gelding was a dream come true for him.

She waved and smiled in greeting, although she would have preferred to drive herself home. She needed time to think. She was concerned about Edee and what it would mean to the widow to have her son home, but more importantly, what it would mean to her when he left. And he would surely leave. Once a young Amish man got a taste of driving pickup trucks, going to the movies and dating *English* girls, they never stayed after a visit with their families.

The buggy rolled to a stop, and she slid open

the door. Sam grinned at her as he stuffed a handful of potato chips from a family-size bag into his mouth. "Hey," he said between bites.

She hesitated. She wanted him to go on without her, and she'd borrow one of the old push scooters in Edee's barn. Instead, she muttered, "Hey, yourself." Climbing into the buggy, she realized she'd left her tote with her work clothes, lunch bag and water bottle at Edee's. "Oh dear," she murmured as she settled on the leather seat beside him.

His smile faded. "What's wrong?"

She closed the door. "Forgot my bag."

"That all?" He wiped his greasy fingers on his pant leg and took the reins in both hands. "We'll get them."

"*Nay*," she exclaimed, laying her hand on his forearm to keep him from giving the gelding the signal to move forward. "No need. It will be there waiting for me tomorrow."

"You sure?" Sam looked down at her. He was an attractive man—at least, that was what her friend Annie told her. Annie even liked his bushy eyebrows. She said they gave him character. Henry had never concerned herself much with a man's looks or anyone else's, including her own. Sam was of average height with curly brown hair, brown eyes and a square jawline that made him look older than his twenty-six years.

"It's no trouble," he told her.

Henry pulled her hand back, not knowing what had possessed her to be so forward with him. They'd been seeing each other for two or three months, but they weren't at the point where she was comfortable with such intimacies. They didn't hold hands or touch casually like she had seen her sisters do. But Millie and Beth had married their beaus, and she suspected that Cora and the new schoolteacher in Honeycomb would announce their betrothal anytime now.

She clasped her hands together on her lap. "Let's go home. I have chores to do, animals to feed, and it's been a long day," she said, not making eye contact with him.

He hesitated and then made a clicking sound between his teeth to urge the horse back onto the road. He hadn't named the gelding, which Henry found odd, and she had told him so. He didn't see any reason to name him and simply called him *my horse*.

"Want some chips?" he asked, indicating the bag between them with a dip of his chin. Crumbs clung to the corners of his mouth. "Spicy barbeque."

"Nay." She shook her head. "Not hungry."

"Long day?"

She stared out the open window as he followed the winding country road. She breathed deeply and exhaled. The spring breeze and warmth of the sun had a calming effect on her. *"Nay,"* she said, turning her attention to him. "It was just...unusual."

"Unusual how? I mean, your days are always unusual, aren't they? Instead of cooking and cleaning or working in your family's store, you're replacing hinges on doors and caulking sinks."

His tone wasn't judgmental. Unlike some of the folks in their community, he wasn't against her having her own home-repair business. He simply couldn't understand why she would want to.

Henry had tried to explain to Sam how important it had been for her to figure out who she was and what to do with herself after her mother died. She'd always been good with her hands, and her father, with seven girls and no boys, had recognized early on her aptitude for tasks traditionally done by males. He taught her how to care for the farm animals, plow behind their Percheron workhorse and repair the blades when necessary. She learned from him how to use a hammer and build a pulley system to raise hay bales into the barn loft as well as any man in Honeycomb.

Henry had loved working with her hands beside her father, and now that he could no longer do many of those things, she treasured the skills he had taught her. To her disappointment, Sam hadn't understood her passion for fixing and building things, and they had both accepted that.

"Let's see," she mused aloud. "I started the morning by shooing a skunk out of Edee's henhouse. That doesn't happen often. Thankfully. Then I had a mishap with a ladder and after that, a stranger showed up at Edee's door." She met his gaze when he glanced at her. "Who turned out *not* to be a stranger at all to Edee. It was her son."

"Whoa!" Sam pulled the dapple gray to a hard stop at a crossroad. "Chandler?" he asked in disbelief.

She drew back in surprise. "You know Chandler Gingerich?"

Sam's eyes widened with wonder beneath the brim of his straw hat. "Wow. Chandler's come home?" He shook his head, gazing out the windshield. "For years I've prayed he'd come back, but I never... I never expected—" He looked at her again. "Edee must be overjoyed."

A minivan stopped behind them, and Sam

urged the horse onto Rose Valley School Road. "I can't believe he's come back to us," he repeated, still in wonder.

"You never mentioned that you knew Chandler," Henry said. "I've been making plans for months to do this renovation for Edee. I see her most days. Why didn't you tell me you knew him?" she asked in exasperation.

The minivan, still behind them, chose that moment to pass the buggy, and Sam held tightly to the reins, speaking gently to his horse until the vehicle flew past them and accelerated away. "You're angry at me."

"I'm not angry at you," she contended. "I just don't understand. You've been dropping me off here for going on two weeks, and you never once mentioned Chandler."

"I didn't mention him because—" He shrugged. "I don't know. I guess because we don't talk about those who've left the church."

"Who doesn't?" she asked, frowning. "Left the Order or not, he was still Edee's son."

Sam stared straight ahead, his tone patient. "In my family, we don't talk about *those* people. They're…dead to us."

She cut her eyes at him. "You shunned him? Edee told me he hadn't even been baptized yet."

"We didn't *shun* him," he said slowly. "We…" He exhaled, which was the closest he ever got to being annoyed with her. "Henny, we've talked about this. My family is different from yours."

She winced at his nickname for her. Her sisters thought it was sweet, at least everyone but Eleanor. Henry didn't like it, and she'd told him so more than once, but either he kept forgetting or didn't care.

"Our family doesn't talk about things like you do," Sam continued. "My *mam* and *dat* aren't modern like Eleanor and your *dat*. My family doesn't take to change easily. They're old-fashioned. They're fine with doing things like we did a hundred years ago."

The idea that her oldest sister, who had taken over running their farm since their mother's death, was a progressive woman made Henry smile. She didn't think of Eleanor that way, but she supposed that in some ways, she was. Because their father had early onset dementia and couldn't run the household or even put on his socks some days, Eleanor had stepped into their mother's shoes and was doing a fine job. At least most of the time. But Eleanor still held on to traditional beliefs, such as that women should train to be wives and find the right man to marry when the time came. That was mostly why Henry had agreed to walk out with Sam in the first place. Eleanor had been pushing her to start thinking about her future, which meant a husband, and it was easier to keep accepting Sam's invitations than quarrel with her sister.

Henry turned on the seat to face Sam. "How do you know Chandler? You grew up in Honeycomb just like me."

"*Nay*, we didn't move to Honeycomb until I was in the sixth grade. And before then, we lived in—"

"Rose Valley," she finished for him, feeling silly that she didn't know that after seeing him for months. But Sam didn't talk much about himself despite her best efforts to learn more about him. His conversations mostly revolved around what had happened at work, what was going on with his family or neighbors and what he had eaten or was going to eat.

"*Ya*. And my grandparents lived next to the Gingerichs, so even after we moved, I saw Chandler all the time. When we got older, we worked for the same construction company for a while before I started apprenticing as a mason." At the next stop sign, he turned right onto Hazlettville Road, moving onto the shoulder because the motor traffic was heavier on the major street. "Is he back for good?"

"I don't know."

"Where's he been all this time? What's he been doing?"

She stared at her clasped hands. "I don't know, Sam."

"I can't believe he didn't come home after his brother died. Why didn't he?"

"I don't know that, either," she answered. "He just arrived."

"You didn't ask him?"

"Sam, I told you. He's just got here." As she continued, her tone became terser. "Edee hasn't seen him in eight years. I wasn't going to interrupt their reunion." She threw up her hands in exasperation. "And I've never met the man. What right do I have to question him?" As the last word burst from her mouth, she lowered her gaze. "I'm sorry," she murmured. "I've no right to raise my voice to you. I just—" She tucked a lock of hair that had fallen across her forehead beneath her prayer *kapp* and let her thought go unfinished.

They were both quiet for a moment. All Henry heard was the rhythmic clip-clop of the horse, the buggy wheels rolling over the pavement and Sam munching on his chips. When she stole a glance at him, he didn't look upset, just…perplexed.

"Are you okay?" he finally asked.

"I'm fine," she muttered. But she wasn't. "I just…" She looked at him again. "Sam, I'm concerned. Why *did* Chandler come back after all this time? Do you think he wants money? Do you think he'll try to take advantage of Edee?"

Sam made a face like she'd just said the most ridiculous thing. "Chandler? Take advantage of his *mudder*? Of course not."

She didn't say anything.

"Henny, he's not that kind of person. I know Chandler. He's a good man."

"Knew," she corrected, watching a motorcycle pass them as it revved its engine loudly.

"What?" Sam had to raise his voice to be heard over the noise. Thankfully, the young driving horse never flinched.

"Knew!" Henry shouted back, cupping her hand around her mouth. Ahead, the motorcycle turned without signaling or stopping at the stop sign, and the sound died away. "You *knew* him," she said, speaking at normal volume again. "You haven't seen him in eight years. You don't know what kind of person he is now."

"I guess I don't," Sam admitted. "But he's here, isn't he? That has to mean something. Maybe he misses being Amish."

"I don't know. Eight years is a long time," she mused aloud, shifting her gaze to the blacktop beneath the dapple gray's hooves. "To be in the *English* world so long, could he ever be satisfied with our Plain ways again?"

Sam eased the buggy to a halt at the stop sign

and glanced at her. "I'm surprised you would say that. You usually have such strong faith, Henny. What if *Gott* brought him home?"

Henry considered his words as they rolled into the intersection and turned left. "I'm not doubting *Gott*, Sam. It's Chandler I have doubts about. It's Edee I fear for." She turned on the seat to face him again. "Sam, Chandler left the church rather than be baptized."

"Right. But many men wrestle with making that final decision. To be baptized is to turn away from the *English* world. It's tempting to a young man." Sam shrugged. "Chandler just made the wrong choice."

She hadn't thought about it that way. She narrowed her gaze, watching him. "Did you consider leaving before you became baptized?"

"Never," he responded firmly. "I've always known exactly who I am and where I belong."

She was surprised by Sam's openness. This was turning out to be the deepest conversation they'd had since the first time he'd asked to give her a ride home from a singing. She tilted her head one way and then the other thoughtfully. "I guess I considered what my life would be if I left the church. Not seriously, but…" She looked at him, wondering if he might not want to admit to his uncertainty. Being baptized into their faith was a huge decision, the biggest an Amish man or woman would ever make. It seemed to her that to *not* question baptism was to enter the covenant blindly, going along with what family, friends and the community asked of you rather than making the decision yourself. "You never had any doubts?"

He shook his head. "None. I was born Amish." They turned off Westville Road, and he gave his horse more rein. The gelding trotted faster. "Back to Chandler. Did he say something that made you think he had returned home for some terrible reason? Did he do something?"

Other than rescuing a stranger from a precarious situation? she thought. But of course she couldn't say that. She had purposefully left out falling off the roof when she'd told Sam about her day because she wanted to avoid discussing his belief that men's work was too dangerous for a woman.

But Sam was right. Chandler Gingerich had not said or done anything wrong.

What about the stranger had unnerved her?

His face flashed before her, and then she knew. It was his handsome smile.

And that worried her.

Henry heard her sisters before she saw them. As she walked past the front door of the family's store, with its Closed sign hanging in a window, laughter rang in the air. She smiled to herself. Hearing her youngest sister's giggles warmed her heart, reminding her that it was time to set her worries aside and enjoy the evening with her family. There was nothing she could do about Chandler. Like it or not, he was at his mother's house, at least for the time being.

She heard another squeal of glee and walked around the corner of the new building to see eighteen-year-old Jane running barefoot through the grass. The hem of her rose-colored dress was wet, and there was another damp spot on her white apron. Behind Jane, their sister Willa sprayed water from a hose at her.

"It's cold!" Jane cried, laughing as she tried to dodge the wet stream.

"I know!" Willa returned, laughing with her. "That's what I told you when you sprayed me!"

"Would you two get back to work and stop wasting water?" Millie chided patiently. Willa's twin knelt in front of a flower bed, where she was planting summer flower bulbs.

The family's general store, which they had only opened the previous year on their property, was making such a profit that they had recently put in a new well and windmill.

When they came up with the idea of building a store that would serve not only their Amish community but *Englishers* as well, it had been a desperate attempt to bring more money into the household. Before their father had been diagnosed with dementia, he had worked in construction and been the primary breadwinner. When he retired, the sisters had all devised ways to support the family financially and make the store possible. They had sold baked goods at the local Amish market, taking in sewing and taught school, and Henry had begun charging for her repair services. Their labor had proven fruitful, and no one in the family was lying awake at night anymore worrying they would lose the family farm.

"Why do you care how much water we use? Eleanor said we dug a deep well and it would last years," Jane argued, wiping a spray of water from her pretty face.

"Because we still shouldn't waste water," Millie responded. "And we need to finish up here so I can get home and fix my husband's supper." She turned her attention to Henry. "Hello, you." Then she looked back to the other two. "You're supposed to be watering the flowers, not yourselves."

Jane stuck her tongue out at Willa, and Willa sprayed her sister again.

Shaking her head, Millie dropped a dahlia bulb into a hole she'd dug in the rich, dark soil.

"See all the fun you miss going off to work?" she asked Henry.

"Want me to do that?" Henry pointed at the flower bulbs. "So you can get home to Elden?" Millie had married their neighbor, and although she had joined her husband's household, the sisters were blessed to see her most days.

"*Nay*. Elden doesn't mind when I get home, so long as I go home to him." She giggled and pulled another bulb from a bright yellow net bag.

Millie was head over heels in love with her husband, and Henry thought it was adorable. Millie had been so worried that no man would ever love her because she was such a big girl. Always heavy for her height. But *Gott* had given her a handsome husband from right next door. Their sister Beth was also a newlywed, and she and her husband Jack lived in an apartment above the store.

"Where's everyone else?" Henry asked, glancing around. In the distance, she saw the family farmhouse and barnyard well off the road where they had built the store.

Millie sat back on her heels and rubbed at a spot of dirt on her chin with the back of her hand. Like Jane, she was barefoot. "Let's see… Cora went to Tobit's to grade essays." Tobit was Cora's beau. "Beth is inside getting the bank deposit for tomorrow together, and *Dat* is supposed to be helping her." She cut her eyes at Henry with amusement. Whenever their *dat* was helping, that usually meant he was causing more work for someone. "And Eleanor took the buggy over to Sara's to deliver supper and a breakfast casserole."

Henry's heart went out to Eleanor's friend Sara and the young woman's entire family. She was a type 1 diabetic, and having two babies in rapid succession had severely affected her health. Sara had been released from the hospital two days ago and was fighting kidney failure. "I wish there was something more we could do than cook meals and watch the little ones for Sara and Jon."

"We can." Millie dug another hole with her trowel. "We can pray for them."

"*Ya*, I know. I pray for them every day," Henry worried aloud. "But that doesn't mean something bad won't happen." As she spoke, she thought of Edee. The older woman desperately wanted her son to return, but that didn't mean it would be a good thing. Sometimes you have to toss out the rotten apples from the basket so it doesn't cause the others to go bad. That was what her aunt Judy said. And she was a bishop's wife, so she knew about these things.

Millie dropped a bulb into the hole she'd dug

and moved over so she wouldn't get sprayed by the water Beth was now directing to the flower bed. Behind Beth, Jane busied herself collecting the net bags filled with tulip bulbs that they had dug up so they could plant the summer bulbs. Their mother had always taken the time to dig up her tulip bulbs, insisting the colors were brighter if they were replanted each fall. None of the sisters had the gift for growing flowers that their mother had possessed, but following in her footsteps as best they could was another way to keep her memory alive.

"Everything all right with you?" Millie asked, gazing up at Henry.

Henry dropped her hands to her hips, unsure she was ready to talk about Chandler. However, experience had taught her that it was always better to share her worries with her sisters than to keep them to herself. So she told Millie about Chandler's homecoming, once again leaving out the detail that she fell from Edee's roof.

"That's wonderful news!" Millie exclaimed, covering up the final bulb before she came to her feet. "I don't know anything about Edee's son other than that he left long ago, but I'm sure folks have been praying for him to return to the fold."

"That sure doesn't happen often," Beth said excitedly as she began to water where her sister had just planted. "His mother must be thrilled to have him home at last for good."

"But that's the point," Henry argued. "You know he's not going to stay. These boys that leave, they don't come back."

"So maybe he's a man now," Jane said, picking up the last of the bags of tulip bulbs.

"What?" Henry asked impatiently. She'd hoped for support when she told her sisters what had happened. She'd thought someone might have even had an idea of how Henry could be sure Chandler really had returned to his family home for the right reasons.

"You said *boys* don't come home," Jane explained, her prayer *kapp* strings bouncing as she spoke. "But maybe he's not a boy anymore. Maybe he didn't feel like he belonged with us as a boy, but now that he's grown into a man, he sees his place in the world. Maybe living with the English made him realize he wants to be Amish."

Henry looked from one sister to the next in frustration. How could they not understand the harm Chandler could cause to his mother? Even if he hadn't come hoping for money, he'd break Edee's heart when he returned to his *English* ways. "How can you not see how terrible this could be for Edee?" she demanded. "Good things don't always happen."

"*Nay*, they don't." Millie slipped her arm around Henry's shoulders. "But sometimes they do, *schweschter*," she murmured. "And that's why we pray. Why we hope, and why we always try to see the good in others."

Henry sighed, suddenly so tired that she felt like she could lie down in the soft spring grass and sleep. "You think I should stay out of it? Do nothing? Say nothing?" She raised her hand and let it fall. "I should do nothing while Chandler takes advantage of his mother—if that's his intention?"

Millie laughed, releasing Henry. "Of course not. You need to pray, to hope, to have faith." She waggled her finger in front of Henry's nose. "And keep an eye on that Chandler."

"Keep an eye on him?" Henry asked, retrieving the trowel and handing it to Millie. "Why me?"

"Because you'll be there working most days, won't you?" Millie narrowed her gaze, her blue eyes sparkling with mischief. "And who better to see what he's up to than our own little spy?"

"I am not a spy," Henry argued, wishing now that she'd never said a word about Chandler.

"Not a spy?" Beth exclaimed, plucking the trowel from Millie's hands and dropping it into the gardening tool pail at their feet. "You were always spying on us and tattling when we were kids."

"I was not."

Beth poked at her with her finger. "What about the time you told *Mam* that Millie was the one who let all the goats out so we could play with them? *Mam* was so mad when the goats ate her favorite tablecloth that she'd hung on the clothesline."

Millie jumped in. "And what about the time you told on us when Beth took the peanut-butter chocolate-chip cookies *Mam* had made for her quilting circle to the loft and ate them all?"

"I did not eat them all," Beth disagreed. "You had some too, Millie."

Millie returned her gaze to Henry. "How hard would it be to watch Chandler? Listen to what he says? You're a good judge of character. You'll soon know if his heart's in the right place."

"Watch him?" Henry repeated incredulously.

"Wait, is he handsome?" Jane asked. She'd recently turned boy crazy as Eleanor liked to say. She was always mooning over someone. Thankfully, still from afar.

Henry looked at her little sister.

"Is Chandler Gingerich handsome?" Jane repeated, then giggled. "Because if he is, it'll be all the easier to watch him."

All three of her sisters laughed in unison, and Henry marched off, headed for the barnyard to start the evening chores. Millie was right, of course. It did make sense for her to keep an eye on Chandler. Edee didn't even have to know. It just exasperated her that first Sam had disagreed with her and now her sisters. In times like this, she felt out of place in the family and truly missed her mother. She had always been different from her sisters, and her *mam* had acknowledged it but promised Henry that she had a place in *Gott*'s world just the same as everyone else in Honeycomb.

Henry prayed it was true.

Chapter Three

Chandler leaned on the handle of a pitchfork and closed his eyes, breathing in the sweet smell of timothy hay and listening to the livestock shift in their stalls as they chewed their morning meal. Of all the things he had missed when he left his family's farm and his faith, this barn was the one he'd most longed for. He'd grown up here among the sacks of grain and bales of straw and hay. He loved the warm, cozy byre that felt like a hug on a chilly morning. He had so many good memories of this place: his sisters squirting milk from a cow's udder at him, his father's laughter at their antics, his brother's kindness in teaching a little brother how to care for their animals.

The thought of Joe made him tear up, and he stabbed at a pile of fresh straw. He couldn't believe he was gone. Gone three years and he hadn't known it. He felt guilty for not knowing, for not coming sooner. But how could he have known his brother had died? Chandler had had no contact with his family since he'd left eight years ago. At least, none other than when he'd sent his mother a birthday card once a year. He'd never included a return address. He'd been so set on not letting his family know where he was that he had often passed the card on to a friend or acquaintance to mail when traveling to another state just to be sure no one could find him.

All these years, he had imagined his brother here on the farm caring for their mother and living the life of a married man. When Chandler left, Joe had been betrothed, and the previous night, his mother confirmed that he and Alma had wed shortly after Chandler left. It had comforted Chandler to imagine his brother married with a flock of little Gingerich children. In his mind, he had seen Joe catching fireflies on a warm night with his little ones and kneeling at the end of the day in the parlor, saying evening prayers. Joe and Alma had had four children, and now Chandler might never meet them because his brother's widow had remarried and moved out of state.

Chandler sniffed and wiped his face on the sleeve of his white T-shirt. He had been so naïve. It had never occurred to him that there may no longer be anyone there on the farm to care for his mother. He had assumed his big brother had stepped into their father's boots—boots Chandler knew he could never have filled. He couldn't imagine his mother's pain after he left and Joe died. First, she lost her husband to pancreatic cancer and her eighteen-year-old son to the *Englishers*. And then, as if that wasn't enough, God had taken her other son.

Chandler flung another pitchfork of clean bedding into the stall the goats had vacated when he'd let them out to pasture. Folks were always saying that God was good. Even his mother said it the previous night when she'd given him the details of Joe's death. She relayed how a cut on his brother's leg had gone septic and taken him in less than a week. Then she'd insisted *Gott* had blessed them by giving the family time to gather around his hospital bed and say goodbye. Joe's wife Alma had placed their four children in bed with their father, and they had prayed and sung hymns as he passed.

How could his mother say such a thing? Did she really believe she was blessed because she had been able to kiss her son's cheek as he died?

He forked the straw faster, his pain turning to anger.

When he'd left, he'd still believed in God, but seeing the world, his faith had waned. It had been his experience in the *English* world that bad things happened to good people all the time, maybe more often than bad people. And there was so much wrongdoing and little respect for others. Maybe it was materialism that led *Englishers* astray. Maybe it was selfishness and the constant desire for gratification. It had certainly led him on many a wrong path over the years. His itch to have a cigarette right now was proof of that.

Seven months ago, he'd given up drinking alcohol, but he only recently quit tobacco. Six days ago, he bumped into a friend of a distant relative in a convenience store in Illinois and heard about Joe's death. Upon learning the news, he'd gone back to his truck without making his purchase. Alone, he'd shakily lit up a cigarette. Smoking, like alcohol consumption, wasn't allowed among the Amish, which was exactly why he had started both after he left home. To turn his nose up at them, as the saying went. That and to fit in better with the *English* guys he worked with.

That day in the store parking lot, he'd taken a long draw on that cigarette, inhaling deeply, and then waited for the nicotine to hit. That was when he realized he wanted to return to Delaware to see his mother. He had contemplated going home many times, but this time he *knew* he would actually go.

Suddenly, the urge to light up a cigarette was dizzying. He wondered if he had a pack under the seat of his truck. It was where he used to keep his carton so his buddies wouldn't steal them. He was overwhelmed by being here without his brother. Would one cigarette be so terrible? A half maybe? Maybe just a puff or two to calm his nerves.

Cigarettes weren't his only addiction, either. He couldn't believe how much he missed the internet. With his cell phone, he could look up anything. He could check the time for a movie, order fast food or read a book. But he'd switched his phone off when he crossed the state line into Delaware and tucked it into the glove compartment of his truck. There was no way his mother would approve of a cell phone or allow one in her home, and he wanted to respect her rules while he was here.

"Chandler!"

His mother's voice made him turn for the huge sliding door he'd closed to keep out the morning chill. And maybe to give himself some time alone. But his *mam* wouldn't be able to hear him from inside.

"Chandler! Chandler, are you here, *sohn*?"

Her voice quavered, and she sounded older than her sixty-eight years.

"Here, *Mam*!" he called, grabbing the door handle with his free hand. "In the barn!" He pushed the heavy paneled door, and it slowly slid aside on its overhead rollers.

"*Ach*, Chandler!" she cried in relief. "There you are."

"Here I am," he said. "I was cleaning stalls. Feeding up. Thought I'd get an early start." He didn't say that he'd slept fitfully in the bedroom he'd once shared with Joe, then had given up all together by four in the morning. There were too many good memories in that little bedroom under the eaves. He had too many regrets to find solace in his dreams.

She rushed toward him. She wore a black bonnet and wool cloak over her dress. A little black handbag hung on her elbow. "*Ach!* You're still here!"

Her words tugged at his heartstrings, and he felt terrible for not leaving a note on the counter. He should have known that if she found him missing from the house, she might think he had left again without saying goodbye. "I told you last night I'd be here for a few days," he said, switching to Pennsylvania *Deitsch*.

There was no reason to speak the only language he'd known until he started attending a one-room schoolhouse at six. His mother spoke English perfectly, but it felt good to say the *Deitsch* words. He'd only allowed himself a few sentences here and there in the time he'd been gone. It was the only way to make the separation between him and his family bearable. Even with others born Amish, he always spoke English.

"You didn't leave," she murmured, tears shining in her eyes as she rushed toward him. When she reached him, she wrapped her arms around his waist and hugged him before she stepped back. "But where is your truck? It's not here. That's why I was afraid you were gone."

He chuckled, mostly because he felt awkward. He didn't remember his mother or father hugging him when he lived here. He had always known they loved him, but there wasn't hugging and kissing among the Amish like with *Englishers*. He liked the hugging and kissing. Even his guy friends hugged each other sometimes.

He leaned on the pitchfork. "I put the truck around back behind the shed. I figured you didn't need it parked next to the house. Otherwise, Anna Jane will be over here wanting to know whose it is." Anna Jane Troyer was one of their neighbors, a busybody who spent a lot of time telling others how they ought to live their lives. But she and his mother were good friends.

His *mam* pressed her lips together and clasped her hands. "Anna Jane died, Chandler. Five years ago. Maybe six, now." She exhaled. "I can't remember. The years seem to be getting away from me."

Chandler's heart tumbled. *Anna Jane had died, too?* It wasn't that he missed the woman, but how awful for his mother. Guilt washed over him in an all-too-familiar wave. He should have been here when Anna Jane died. He should have been here when Joe died.

Glancing away, he cleared his throat. "Where are you off to so early?" He nodded, indicating her going-to-town clothes.

"Doctor's appointment."

"You *oll recht*?"

"*Ya*. Just a checkup. Keeping an eye on my cataracts." She glanced in the direction of the road. "My driver ought to be here any minute."

"Driver?" He set the pitchfork against a support beam. "You don't need a driver. I can take you in my truck."

She shook her head. "Already reserved. I'd have to pay Angela whether I go or not. She's my driver. A no-nonsense woman. Used to teach high school before she retired. But she charges if you don't cancel a day ahead. It's how things are these days. Not enough drivers. Too many Amish women not feeling safe driving their buggies in town. Too much traffic. Too many *farukt* drivers. Crazy, they are." She glanced at the road again. "I left breakfast for you in the oven. Just in case you were still here."

"Mam," he said gently. "I'm still here, just like I promised. And I won't leave without telling you. Not this time," he added. *Never again.*

"Ham and eggs and hotcakes," she said as if she hadn't heard him. Except that he knew she had. "You always liked my buckwheat hotcakes," she continued. "Maple syrup is in the refrigerator."

"I know where you keep the syrup," he answered gently. "And if I didn't, I could manage to find it. I've been making my own breakfast for years."

"Butter and honey on the counter in the pantry," she went on. "I get honey from a woman over in Seven Poplars, Johanna Byler. One of Hannah Yoder's girls. You remember them? Nice family. The husband died, and Hannah was left to raise her girls alone. But she did a fine job. Married 'em all off and found a husband herself."

He squinted, trying to recall the family. "I

don't know if I remember them. It's been a long time, *Mam*."

"*Ach!* There she is!" His mother hurried down the driveway as fast as her small feet and bad knees could carry her. "Eat your breakfast! I won't be long."

He waved to her as she hustled down the driveway and thought to himself, *it's good to be home*.

Henry said goodbye to Sam and walked up Edee's driveway carrying a paper lunch sack. As she entered the barnyard, she was disappointed not to see Chandler's white truck. But she wasn't surprised.

Poor Edee, she thought. *She must be heartbroken.* Henry couldn't believe he hadn't stayed even a full day. She frowned as she walked up the porch steps, where Edee's old collie greeted her.

"Hey, girl." Henry stroked the dog's head. "Where's Edee?" she asked. "Is she inside? Is she, old girl?"

The collie wagged her tail enthusiastically.

Henry missed having a dog. Theirs had passed away a couple of years ago, and Eleanor had put her foot down about getting another. Ellie insisted a puppy was too much work and she'd end up caring for it. Their *dat* loved dogs—was obsessed with them—and wanted one, but so far he hadn't been able to budge his eldest daughter on the matter. Instead, he made himself content spending time with his son-in-law Elden's bulldog.

Henry gave the collie one more pat, knocked on the door and walked in. "Edee!" she called. "I'm here." Inside the mudroom, she wiped her feet on the mat, hung her jacket on a hook and walked into the kitchen. "Edee?" She carried her lunch bag to the refrigerator.

She didn't see Edee, but she did see that the upper cabinets to the left of the stove had been emptied. The doors were open, and on the counter rested tools that someone would use to take them off the wall. Not *someone*. *Chandler*. Who else would have done it?

She felt the heat of anger wash across her cheeks. "Edee?" she repeated, her tone sharper.

Footsteps sounded in the hallway. But not Edee's.

"She's not here," came a male voice. And then he walked into the kitchen. It was Chandler, dressed in a tight white T-shirt, faded blue jeans and work boots. "Doctor's appointment."

Henry stared at the wall cabinets that had seen better days, their doors flung open. "What do you think you're doing?"

"Sorry?" He walked to the stove and picked

up a coffee pot that had been percolating. "Coffee?" He held up the battered pot she knew had belonged to Edee's mother.

She shook her head, looking from him to the cabinets and back at him again.

"Breakfast?" Chandler asked as if there was nothing wrong. "*Mam* made enough hotcakes, eggs and ham to feed the county." He patted his stomach. "I had two helpings of each, but I can't eat another thing. It's still warm in the oven."

"I had breakfast at home, *danki*," she answered tersely. She pointed at the cabinets. "What are you doing?"

He poured himself a mug of coffee. "What do you mean?"

She pointed again, this time her movement jerky. She knew exactly what he was doing. He was trying to take over her renovation project. He was trying to steal her first big job. But she wanted to hear him say it.

"*Ya*, what are you doing with the cabinets?" she demanded.

He glanced at them, then his gaze settled on her. He leaned casually against the sink. "*Mam* told me she's wanted to renovate her kitchen for years." He glanced around. "These were the cabinets that were here when we moved in when I was a kid." He frowned. "Terrible quality. They're basically pressed paper. I'm a carpenter. I build cabinets and install them, among other things, so I will put them in for her."

"*Ya*, Edee does want her kitchen renovated. Which is why *I'm* doing it," she blurted.

The moment the words were out of her mouth, she wished she could take them back. What if Edee had changed her mind and asked her son to do it? she wondered. What if it was a tactic to keep him here longer? Could she blame Edee if it was? But Henry would be devastated if she lost the job. She'd worked months planning the project. She knew she was being selfish to feel this way, but she couldn't help it.

She took a step toward Chandler, trying to remain calm. "Your mother hired me," she said firmly. "I'll be doing the work."

He tucked a lock of chin-length blond hair behind his ear and took another drink of his black coffee. "You're a *contractor*?"

He didn't have to say what he meant. He was questioning the idea that a *woman* could do the work.

"*Ya*," she said. "Mostly, I do repair work for women in the community who live alone, but I guess I am a contractor now. I have a business license." She folded her arms over her chest.

"And you're full-on Amish, right?" he asked, still studying her. "Not Mennonite?"

Full-on Amish. She'd never heard that one

before. She supposed he learned that from the *English*. "*Ya*, full-on Amish."

"And what's your husband got to say about you doing this kind of work?"

She drew back, further annoyed that he thought she was the kind of woman who would allow a husband to make decisions for her. Sadly, his assumption wasn't unfounded. Many Amish women lived in households where the men made all the decisions. But that wasn't the way she had been brought up. Her father may have been the head of the household regarding their religious upbringing, but her parents had made decisions together. They'd always consulted each other on matters large and small.

"My *husband*?" Henry asked, her anger rising again. "What makes you think I'm married?"

For the first time, his easygoing nature changed. Now he looked uncomfortable. "You're not married?"

"No. What made you think I was?"

"I don't know. I just—" He set his mug on the counter. "Yesterday afternoon, *Mam* said someone named Samuel was picking you up." He shrugged. "I assumed Samuel was your husband. He's not your husband?"

She shook her head.

"Betrothed?" When she didn't respond, he said, "Beau?"

"Nope," she told him. Which maybe wasn't completely honest, but she'd not agreed to officially walk out with him, so he wasn't officially her boyfriend. "Neighbor," she told him. She pointed across the room. "Back to the cabinets. Did Edee ask you to start pulling them down?"

"No," he said slowly. He looked at them and then back at her. "But I thought it would be nice to get started. She told me she'd ordered new ones from the wood shop in Seven Poplars, so I thought—"

"You thought you'd take my job from me," she interrupted.

"No...well...yes." He scratched his head. "I mean, I thought maybe I could do the renovation for her. I work construction for a living. I'm on a crew that builds houses back in Illinois. I do mostly trim, hardwood floors, some interior framing, when need be, but—"

"No," Henry said harshly, her voice getting louder with each word she spoke. "You are *not* going to take my job, and you're *not* going to make your mother think you're going to stick around when you know very well—"

The sound of the back door opening startled Henry, and she fell silent, her eyes widening in surprise.

"Chandler! Henry! What's going on in here?" Edee called. "What's all the shouting?"

Chandler raised his eyebrows, cutting his eyes at Henry. "Now look what you've done," he whispered.

Chapter Four

Edee walked into the kitchen still wearing her bonnet and cloak, a large brown paper sack in her arms. "I said, what's going on in here?"

Against her will, tears stung Henry's eyes. She was embarrassed she had nearly gotten into a shouting match with her friend's son and the widow had heard it. She'd lose her job now for sure.

"No one's shouting, *Mam*." Chandler picked up his mug, his tone casual. "Henry and I were having a discussion. You know how I am. I have strong opinions. Seems Henry does, too." He sipped his coffee. "What are you doing back so soon?"

Now, on top of being embarrassed, Henry felt uncomfortable. Why was Chandler covering for her? And the way he had said *strong opinions*... It hadn't come off as being critical. It sounded like a compliment.

Edee looked suspiciously at Henry and then

at Chandler. "My appointment got rescheduled," she said slowly. "The doctor's office called when we were halfway there. I'd have been home sooner, but we stopped at Byler's so I could pick up a few things."

"They called you?" Chandler lowered his mug. "Called you how?"

Edee pursed her lips. "On my cell phone, *sohn*. How do you think?" She moved to set the groceries down, but Henry took them from her to give herself something to do with her hands. She regretted letting this man rile her and felt shame hot on the back of her neck.

"You have a cell phone?" he asked, clearly surprised.

Edee whipped off her bonnet. "I'm an old, widowed woman living alone. It would be foolish of me *not* to have a cell phone these days."

"I can't believe you have a phone," Chandler mused aloud. "You used to say you'd never have one of those contraptions in your house."

"*Ach!* People change. Like it or not, our world has changed. And it's not as if I sit around all day chatting on it. I only have it for emergencies and to call doctors and such." She shook her head. "Now what's going on here?" She set her bonnet on the old walnut table that easily sat eight. "Between the two of you." She pointed at her son and then at Henry.

Henry began to remove items from the bag.

Chandler eyed Henry before he returned his attention to his mother. "A misunderstanding is all. I was going to take the old cabinets down for you. Start repairing the walls so they can be painted before the new cabinets go in. You said they should be ready in the next few weeks." He looked up at the ceiling, where there was a big brown stain. "It looks like you had a leak at some point. Thought I'd have a look at that, too. Make sure nothing's rotted up there. You don't want the bathtub coming through the ceiling of your new kitchen. The repair will take a few days with letting the spackling dry, but I've got the time."

"You're *staying*?" Edee murmured.

Did he intend to stay? Henry was as stunned as his mother sounded. She sneaked a peek at him.

"*Mam*, I told you—" He halted, then started again. "Can we not talk about this right now?" He brushed his shaggy blond hair out of his eyes. "I was trying to do something nice for you."

Edee took her time removing her cloak. "I told you last night that I hired Henry to renovate my kitchen and pantry."

"No. What you *said* was that Henry was helping you out. I thought that meant... I don't know…that she was emptying cabinets, helping you clean up once everything's been torn out. Something along those lines. I didn't know she did construction work."

Because he thinks a woman can't hang cabinets or repair a ceiling, Henry thought with annoyance.

"I'm sorry I wasn't clear, *sohn.* I hired Henrietta here to renovate my kitchen." There was suddenly a stubbornness in Edee's tone. "Because I have *no family* to do it for me."

Chandler faced his mother, and Henry was surprised that she felt sorry for him. She saw regret for hurting his mother on his face and in the slump of his shoulders.

"I'm here now, *Mam*," he said. His first words were weak, but gained strength as he continued. "And I want to help. I want to do this for you."

Edee dropped her cloak over the back of one of the mismatched chairs at the table. "But I hired Henry to do it."

He gestured to Henry. "Pay her for her work and let me do the rest."

"It's easily a month of work, maybe more," Edee said slowly. "I thought you had to return to your Illinois job."

A lump rose in Henry's throat as she turned her back on them and began to stack cans of corned beef hash and soup. *She was going to lose her job.*

Edee would have her son renovate her kitchen to keep him here. Henry wasn't angry at Edee for her choice. She'd do the same thing if she were in Edee's shoes. Any woman would do anything to bring a lost child back into the fold. But that didn't mean it didn't hurt. Accepting this job had been hard on Henry and maybe harder on her family. So many folks in Honeycomb disapproved of her doing what they saw as a man's job. And then when they learned she was going into the contracting business, some had even become angry. Folks worried she would steal work from a man with a family to support, which made no sense because she only did jobs for women like Edee. More than once, her mother's sister, Judy, wife of their bishop, had come to the house to talk to Eleanor about the mistakes she was making by letting her younger sisters run wild. And there was always a discussion about how inappropriate it was for Henry to be doing what she did. Henry had considered giving it up, but she truly felt she had a calling to help these women.

"Would you stay long enough to finish the job?" Edee asked her son.

Chandler hesitated, maybe fearing to commit, Henry thought.

"I would, *Mam*," he said at last.

"But what about your job?"

"I can call my boss and let him know I'm staying with you for a while. He's a good guy. When I told him about Joe, he said to take as much time as I needed here. He said I was a hard worker, good at what I did, and I'd always have a job with him." He picked up his mug and carried it to the sink to wash it.

"Henry, could I speak to you?" Edee asked. When Henry looked at her, the widow cut her eyes at her son, whose back was to them. "Just the two of us?"

"Of course," Henry answered. What else was she going to say? She and Edee had become friends, and she liked and admired the older woman. She'd do anything for her, even give up a job she wanted, if that was what Edee needed.

Henry followed her from the kitchen into one of the two identical parlors. Decades ago, when the family moved there, Edee's husband had widened the arched doorways to both rooms directly across the hall from each other. That way, when the family took their turn hosting church, they could use both parlors and the hall as a single chamber, and at least a dozen large families could attend services.

As soon as the two women stepped into the parlor, Edee turned to Henry. "I don't know what to do," the widow said quietly. She was upset. "Chandler says he'll stay to fix up my kitchen."

Henry wasn't sure how to respond. She was still worried that he was here to take advantage of her. If she said nothing, wouldn't she be partially responsible if he was just here for money? She nibbled on her lower lip. "Edee, he's been living the life of an *Englisher*. You have no idea what sort of things he's been doing. What sins he's committed."

"I do not," she agreed. "And I don't care. Chandler was never baptized. Don't you know the story of the prodigal son? No matter what he's done, I must welcome him back."

"But what if he... What if Chandler isn't here for the right reasons? What if he wants something from you?" Henry asked.

"Like what?"

Henry hesitated, then said, "Money?"

Edee smiled at her as if she were a child. "I haven't much money, but he's welcome to what I have. I don't care about money. I care about my son. I care about him getting into heaven someday. But I must have him here to help him see there's still time to save himself. I think that kitchen could keep him here."

Henry stared at her steel-toed work boots peeking from beneath her dress. "You don't have a choice, then, Edee," she said softly. "You have to let him do it."

"But I hired you." The older woman pressed her hand to her forehead. "You drew up all the plans and got the permits. You helped me pick out the cabinets. You've been so patient with me for months. And...and I signed a contract with you."

Henry smiled, touched that her friend would consider her feelings. "I don't care about the silly contract, Edee. I only wrote that because I thought it was what I should do. This was my first renovation job, and I wanted to do things right." She took one of Edee's veined, wrinkled hands in hers. "You have to let Chandler do it so he'll stay."

Edee sighed. "So *maybe* he'll stay." She looked up at Henry. "But for how long?"

Henry squeezed the widow's hand and released it. "I don't know. But the longer he's here, the more opportunity there is to talk with him and convince him that he belongs here with you. That *we're* his folks. That this is his world, here among the Plain people." She raised her chin. "Not out there."

"You think there's a chance that could happen? That he could return to us?"

When Henry looked at Edee, she saw tears sparkling in the woman's gray eyes. "I don't know, but how will you know if you don't try? I think that's your duty as a mother, don't you? I know I'm not a mother, but I'd do anything to save my child if I were."

Edee exhaled thoughtfully. "You're right. I know you are. It's only that I..." She exhaled again. *"Oll recht."*

Without another word, Edee walked out of the parlor. Henry followed, thinking about what work she could dig up for the following week. If she didn't find some odd jobs until she formulated a new plan, she'd have no choice but to offer to take shifts at the family store. It wasn't that she minded working in the family business. What she minded was having to run the cash register and make small talk with their *English* customers. People were never satisfied to talk about the weather or how sweet the season's strawberries were this year. They wanted to talk about personal things. They asked the rudest questions that quickly got on her nerves.

Henry walked into the kitchen behind Edee. *"Oll recht, sohn,"* the widow announced. "I've decided you can do the work on my kitchen."

Chandler turned from the sink, which he was rinsing out. "That's great news," he said, sounding excited. "Don't worry. You won't regret it. I'm good at this, *Mam*. You'll see. I'll get started right away. Today." He hesitated and then added, "It's right that I should do this for you."

I guess I should pack up my tools and be on my way, Henry thought, glumly trying not to be too disappointed. Because although this wasn't good for her, it was good for Edee. And maybe good for her son, even if he didn't know it yet. So she'd pack up her tools today and return in the family buggy in a day or two to pick them up.

"You're right, *sohn*," Edee continued. "You should stay here and fix up your widowed mother's kitchen. As much worry and gray hair as you've given me, you owe me as much." She smiled. "And I know that Henry will appreciate your help."

Chandler whipped around from the sink, still holding the faucet sprayer. Water squirted across the faded linoleum floor. "What?" He quickly released the sprayer and grabbed a towel to mop up the water.

"You heard me." Edee picked up her cloak and bonnet. "You offered to do up my kitchen, and I accept your offer. I can't go back on my agreement with Henry, of course, but there's no reason why you can't help her out. Another set of hands and all that. *Ya?*" She glanced at Henry.

Henry knew she must have looked ridiculous standing there, her mouth gaping wide open in surprise. It was a good thing there were no flies in the kitchen, or one might have flown into it.

"Will you let my son here help you with the job?" Edee asked. "Because if you don't want him to help, he can be on his way. He can go back to his life in Illinois."

Henry didn't know what to say for a moment. She closed her mouth. Of course, she didn't want Chandler's help. She wanted to do this on her own. She wanted her family, friends and neighbors to know she could do it. But she couldn't say that, could she? Not after she'd just told Edee it was her responsibility as a mother to do anything she could to keep her son here.

"*Ya*," Henry managed. "Of course. An extra set of hands will be nice." She met Chandler's gaze and saw that he wasn't any happier about the new arrangement than she was.

And that made her smile.

"The matter's settled, then," Edee declared. "Now I've got work to do and so do you. I'm off to hang the laundry on the line." She headed for the mudroom with her cloak and bonnet. "That one"—she nodded in Chandler's direction—"was in such a hurry to get here that he only packed one pair of pants and a shirt," she told Henry as she walked by.

"Two shirts," Chandler corrected.

"A good thing I've got an automatic washer that runs on propane. Not like that ringer I had when my boys werelittle," Edee continued as she walked out of the kitchen. "Looks like I'm going to be washing a lot."

Henry watched the widow go, pressing her lips together to keep from smiling or, worse, laughing. When Edee was gone from the room, she looked at Chandler.

He met her gaze. "Not exactly how I saw things going," he said.

"Me either," Henry agreed, feeling a bit smug now. Something she wasn't proud of. But it did feel good to know that Edee had enough confidence in her to let her still oversee the project.

"But I shouldn't be surprised. This sounds like something my mother would do," he told her.

Henry noticed that he didn't sound angry. Didn't *look* angry, and that intrigued her. It wasn't the response she expected, and that said something about his character. She considered saying so but decided it was probably best to get to work and let it go. She'd never had anyone work for her before, so she didn't know how to do it. Did she ask him where he wanted to start or what he wanted to do, or did she tell him what to do? She contemplated that briefly, then decided to pretend Chandler was one of her sisters and they were set to a task like she'd done thousands of times with them.

"I'm going to put these groceries away and get changed," she said. "I'm thinking we pull these upper cabinets down first. Why don't you get started on that."

He nodded, looking up at them. "Good plan, boss."

As she picked up two stacks of cans, she felt her cheeks grow warm. Of course, that was the best place to start. He'd already figured that out. "You don't have to call me that."

"But that's what I call my boss on the job-site."

She couldn't tell by his tone if he was laughing at her. She whipped around. "Look, I know you don't think I can do this. That I should be "

"I never said that," he interrupted. "I've worked with two different women on job crews. One in Indiana and one in Illinois. This one woman, Amber, she's the best drywaller my boss knows. Works with her dad and brother. You should see her on those stilts. She's faster than they are."

"Really?" Henry asked, looking up at him, the canned goods still in her hands. "*Englishers* don't mind having women on work crews?" She looked up at him and noticed for the first time that he had pale blue eyes that almost looked gray.

"I wouldn't go so far as to say that. Want me to take those?" He pointed at the cans she was balancing.

She shook her head no.

"Some men don't like it," he went on. "Bruises their egos, I guess. You know, they think construction is a man's job, and they don't want to take the chance of getting bettered by a girl."

Something about his eyes made her want to keep looking into them. "Does your ego bruise easily?" she asked him.

His mouth twitched in a lazy smile. "I don't know." He walked away. "I'll let you know in a few days."

At three forty-five that afternoon, Henry called the day done. She excused herself from the kitchen to change clothes and left Chandler to clean up any mess they'd made so Edee could make supper in her kitchen. Henry intended not to interfere in the widow's daily routine more than she had to. Plus, she wouldn't be back until Monday morning because it was Friday.

Henry thought about her day as she donned a dress and prayer *kapp* in the bathroom and exchanged her work boots for black canvas sneakers. It had certainly started rocky. Eight hours ago, she thought she'd lost the job. Then had come the surprise that, whether she liked it or not, she'd have an extra set of hands to help her with the renovation. But once the matter of who would oversee the renovation had been settled, she'd been surprised by how well the rest of the day had gone.

When she had gone along with the widow's decision to have Chandler help her with the project, Henry assumed he would be resentful. He had acted as if he didn't care, but she'd still thought he wouldn't make it easy for her. Within an hour, however, she had figured out that Chandler was content to take direction from her and was extremely capable. She'd also discovered that she liked him, though she was reluctant to admit it.

Henry found that idea disquieting for multiple reasons. The fact that he had threatened her job didn't matter to her now. To use one of Chandler's *Englisher* phrases, *she was over that*. What worried her now was how much he had hurt Edee by leaving the Old Order Amish and staying away so long. And when he left, he would hurt his mother all over again. She also didn't want to like him because he wasn't Amish. He was *English* now, which meant he didn't believe in her way of life. And there was the matter of his life as an *Englisher*. How could his morals not have been affected by a life of half-naked women in the grocery stores and on TV? How could he not have strayed from Amish beliefs while surrounded by rock music, alcohol, tobacco and worse?

She sighed as she dropped her work boots and clothes into her tote bag. Sam would be at the door if she didn't hurry, and then their return to Honeycomb would be delayed while he chatted with Chandler. She didn't intend to keep the two apart but wanted to get away from Chandler with his easygoing nature and handsome smile.

Henry picked up her bag, and on her way out, glanced into a tiny mirror on the wall. Like most Amish homes, there was no large mirror over the sink or on the back of the door. Mirrors, while maybe not sinful, had a way of encouraging vanity, so they were avoided. That didn't mean a woman couldn't have a small mirror to be used to be sure her prayer *kapp* was properly in place and her hair covered decently.

Henry caught her reflection in the mirror, and satisfied that even her uncle the bishop would approve, she headed down the hall.

"You sure you won't stay for supper?" Edee asked as Henry entered the kitchen.

"*Danki*, but no." Henry gave a quick smile. Some days, she stayed to eat with the widow to keep her company, but not tonight. She'd spent quite enough time with Chandler already. She wanted to go home, where she was most comfortable. She needed to ground herself by breaking bread with her family and listening to her sisters argue, laugh and discuss their day.

"Come now, I know Chandler and I would enjoy your company." Edee opened the oven door to check on a chicken she was roasting. "I don't know any young man who wouldn't enjoy conversation with a young lady more than his old mother."

"*Mam*, she said no," Chandler chided, carrying a large black trash bag out of the pantry. He eyed Henry as he spun the bag and secured it. "I imagine she's had enough of us for the day."

"I'll be on my way." Henry flashed another smile, this time in their general direction. "Have a good weekend."

"I'll walk you down," Chandler said, falling in behind her.

She glanced over her shoulder. She hadn't expected that. "I…there's no need for you to walk me down. I think I can find the road."

"It's a turn of phrase. I didn't mean I was

actually walking you down," Chandler said, amusement in his voice. He held up the black garbage bag. "I'm going to toss this in the dumpster. *Mam* said they don't usually pick up until five."

Henry felt a blush of embarrassment for what seemed like the hundredth time with this man. What about him so easily made her uncomfortable? "Bye, Edee," she called, hurrying out of the kitchen.

Henry and Chandler walked side by side down the lane in silence. The cool spring breeze felt refreshing after a day of working inside, and she breathed deeply. As they continued, she felt like she should say something, but even though they'd been working and talking together all day, she suddenly felt self-conscious. Thankfully, he spoke first.

"I think that went pretty well today." Chandler swung the heavy bag as he walked. "I think we can work together and get *Mam*'s kitchen the way she wants it. How about you?"

"It went well enough." She felt his gaze on her and glanced up.

"Come on. Admit it." There was a teasing tone to his voice. "It wasn't as terrible as you thought it would be, being forced to hire a helper."

"I didn't hire you," she warned, unable to

resist a smirk. "Edee made that clear. I'm not supposed to pay you, so if you expect a check next Friday, you'll be sorely disappointed."

Chandler laughed and tugged on the brim of the baseball hat he'd pulled onto his head as they went out the door. "I wasn't talking about a paycheck, and you know it. Admit it, you were afraid we couldn't work together."

"I wouldn't say that," Henry responded. "It's only that I've never worked with anyone else. Well, I do take my *dat* with me sometimes. He's harder to work with than you are, I'll give you that."

"Why's that? Not good with his hands?" Chandler moved the heavy garbage bag to his other hand. "I assumed he was the one who taught you how to use the claw on a hammer the way you do."

When she looked at him, he was smiling at her.

"It's complicated," she said. With relief, she spotted Sam's buggy approaching on the road. "*Ach.* There's my ride. I guess I'll see you Monday."

"I'll be here," he answered as he crossed the driveway to where the trash receptacle stood.

Sam eased his buggy off the road, the wheels crunching on the gravel, and Henry reached for the door the moment he stopped. She knew the two men had been friends, but she wasn't up to a reunion right now. She was fine with Sam visiting on his own as he told her he would, but she didn't want to be a part of it. Besides, she needed to tell Sam that she and Chandler were going to work together. Or rather Chandler was going to work for her, and she wasn't certain she was up for that conversation tonight.

"Have a good weekend," Chandler called.

When she looked back at him, she saw him drop the bag into the dumpster as he squinted to see into the buggy.

"Hey, is that Sam Yoder?" Chandler asked. "Johnny and Martha Yoder's Sam?"

"Ya," she admitted. "It is."

Chandler hurried after her. "Why didn't you say so? Why didn't my *mam* say so? Sam and I were pals when we were kids." He sounded excited. "Sam!"

Henry stepped out of his way as Chandler thrust his head into the buggy.

"Chandler!" Sam's face lit up as he wrapped the reins around the handbrake and climbed across the bench seat.

Fighting a sense of annoyance, she stood back, her tote dangling on her elbow.

"So good to see you!" Sam jumped out of the buggy, licking crumbs from his fingers. "When Henny told me you were here visiting your *mam*, I couldn't believe it." He grinned, giving Chandler a friendly push on the shoulder. "It's so good to see you. I planned on calling on you tomorrow, but here you are."

"Here I am," Chandler agreed, seeming as genuinely happy to see Sam as he was him.

"You staying a few days?" Sam asked. He glanced at Henry, then back at Chandler. "Be nice to talk, but I've got to get Henny home. And I promised to help *Dat* with the milking. His gout's acting up again. But we should get together sometime."

"I'd like that." Chandler tugged on his ball-cap again.

As Henry stepped up through the open door of the buggy, hoping to move Sam along, he said, "Hey, I've got an idea. Henny and I are going to a singing at my brother's place. We're going to play volleyball. They live down the road from here. Want to join us? That would be all right, *ya*, Henny?" He threw a glance over his shoulder. "If Chandler goes with us?"

Henry pushed aside a half-eaten bag of sour cream and onion potato chips and dropped onto the leather seat. Of course, she didn't want Chandler to go on their date with them, but how could she say no to that? The men were old friends and hadn't seen each other in years.

"Come on," Sam urged Chandler. "It will be fun, right, Henny?"

Chandler met her gaze, then shifted his attention to Sam. "Okay. Sure."

"*Goot.* Great." Sam grinned as he closed Henry's door. "We'll be by to pick you up around five." As he walked in front of his horse, he patted the gelding on his withers.

"Sounds good." Chandler raised his hand in farewell.

Henry rode silently beside Sam, listening to him crunch on his chips until they reached the first stop sign. Suddenly she looked at him. "You invited your friend on our date?" she blurted.

In the order of things, young men taking young women home from an outing like the one they were going to wasn't considered anything too serious. It wasn't a date. It was how men and women spent time together to get to know each other well enough to see if they were interested in dating. However, casual dating quickly became serious business among the Old Order Amish. Dating was meant to lead to betrothal and then to marriage. Unless a girl was a serial dater like Henry's sister Willa, once folks knew a couple was dating, questions started circulating about when the couple would be making an appointment with their bishop to discuss the intention of marriage. That was one of the reasons Henry wasn't ready for people to think she was dating Sam.

"What's that?" Sam clicked between his teeth, and the gelding trotted through the intersection.

Henry sighed loudly. "I'm asking why you invited someone on our date."

His grin was lopsided. "Ah, so now it *is* a date. When I offered to pick you up, you said it wouldn't be a date. Now it is?"

Ignoring his question, she stared straight ahead. One of Edee's neighbors, driving matching Percherons, was pulling a wagon of manure down the road, and motor traffic was backing up behind him. "Why would you invite someone to join us after you said we weren't seeing enough of each other and you wanted to talk, just the two of us?"

"Henny, Chandler was my best friend."

"I know that."

"I want to catch up. And he might enjoy playing some volleyball. He was always good at it. Better than me."

Henry worked her jaw with annoyance. She had half a mind to tell Sam to take Chandler to the singing instead of her. But that would be unkind, and she wasn't an unkind person. She wasn't normally a suspicious person, either. So far, nothing Edee's son had said or done suggested he was anything more than what he appeared to be—a young man home visiting his mother after learning of a tragedy their family had suffered.

She turned to Sam. "You're right."

"I am?" He sounded surprised.

"*Ya.* It was the right thing to do, inviting Chandler. It'll be nice for the three of us to go together." If nothing else, it would keep Sam from trying to corner her into agreeing to court. She wasn't ready for that.

She wasn't sure she would ever be.

Chapter Five

Chandler stood beside Sam and sipped an orange pop as they watched Henry and her friends play volleyball. The sun had set and his buddy's sister-in-law, Mary Aaron, had declared this match would be the last. The single men and women who gathered for the singing had been playing for two hours, and he'd enjoyed participating as well as watching. As goofy as it would have sounded to his work friends in Illinois, he'd missed this kind of wholesome fun. An evening spent on an Amish farm enjoying games meant no one drank too many beers, got sick or started a fistfight over who would sit with a particular woman on the tailgate of his truck.

The volleyball games were played the same way they had been played eight years ago. First, it had been guys against guys, then guys against girls, and now the women were playing each other. Mary Aaron had announced that once this game ended, they'd have something to eat and then there would be singing and a short Bible lesson with a reading led by her husband. According to Sam, his brother saw himself becoming a preacher someday. Enos liked practicing, so he took every opportunity to share a message. That was one of the reasons he and his wife often held singings for the young, unmarried Amish folks in the county.

Chandler couldn't believe he'd almost missed out on the fun. Earlier in the day, he'd considered canceling on Sam. It was kind of his buddy to invite him, but he doubted Henry wanted to work with him *and* see him off-hours. He'd figured he could easily use his mother as an excuse, saying he wanted to spend as much time with her as he could while in town. As it had grown closer to five o'clock, he'd almost been desperate for an excuse not to go because singings were one of the reasons he'd left the Amish community in the first place. It wasn't so much the actual events that bothered him. It was the purpose of these occasions that he didn't like. While everyone in Amish communities spoke of the importance of young adults socializing, the true reason for these gatherings was for singles to find spouses, and everyone knew it. Chandler had hated the idea that his only worth in his community had been to marry and produce more Amish children.

He'd also been uncomfortable with singing the hymns he had grown up with. And then there were the Bible lessons. He hadn't been to a church service or sung in High German since he left home. Over the years, a few Amish guys had invited him to join them for Sunday services, and quite a few Mennonite buddies had reached out to him about attending their church, but he had never gone. He'd abandoned his faith when he walked off the farm and figured he had no right to listen to God's word. But maybe he'd been overthinking the whole thing. He was actually having an okay time, maybe even a good one.

Chandler didn't know many people at the gathering because most of the people he used to hang around with were married and no longer attended singings. He'd been surprised by how nice it was to reconnect with families he'd grown up with. And while a few folks hadn't been particularly friendly, most ignored his blue jeans, white T-shirt, Nike sneakers and ballcap and welcomed him as if *Englishers* joined them all the time. And Henry seemed fine with him being there. When she and Sam arrived to pick him up, she'd greeted him with a smile and climbed into the back of the buggy so he could sit up front. She hadn't contributed much to the conversation on the way to Sam's brother's house, but he'd found it strangely comforting to have her nearby.

"I know your *mam* must be happy to have you home," Sam said casually, bringing Chandler back to the present.

"She is," Chandler agreed, his gaze straying to Henry. He watched her serve the ball, and he smiled. She had a great serve. It was bold and confident, just like she was. Not something he usually associated with Amish women.

"So I guess you'll stick around for a while, *ya*?"

Chandler shrugged. "Long enough to do my mother's renovation." He glanced at his friend. "I assume Henry filled you in on all that? Us working together."

"A bit. She said it was what your *mam* wanted. I was glad to hear it. You being in construction and all. This way Henny can still feel like she's doing something for Edee, but you can take charge."

Chandler was about to take another drink of his pop but lowered the can. "Oh, I'm not in charge. This is Henry's job. I'm only helping out. My mother made that very clear."

Sam looked so perplexed by that information that Chandler went on. "*Mam* had already given her the contract before I arrived. It's only fair Henry do the work."

"But *you're* here now," Sam said.

Chandler shouldn't have been surprised by Sam's response. His friend had always been good at being Amish. He never questioned things. Never looked for change, never wanted it. "But it's still Henry's job," he said. "So far, she seems to know her stuff. She told me there were a lot of things she'd be doing for the first time, but she knows what she needs to know so far, and she's good at it. She has a sharp mind and isn't afraid to ask questions. She did a lot of planning and reading before she got started. I've every confidence she could do this work without me."

Sam frowned as if still trying to wrap his head around the whole thing. "And you don't mind taking orders from, you know, a girl?"

"You mean a woman?" Chandler asked, raising his eyebrows.

Among the Amish, *girl* and *boy* were often used until marriage. Only then were they men and women, but at twenty-six years old, he didn't like being called a boy, and when he looked at Henry, he certainly didn't see a girl. He took another drink. "No, Sam, I don't mind working for a woman. It's not that way in the *English* world." He motioned with the can. "Out there, women are doctors, pilots, electricians, lumberjacks, you name it."

Those standing around the volleyball court broke into applause and shouts of encouragement, and Chandler looked up. Henry was still serving, and it was game point. "So... I'm a little confused about you and Henry," he said, changing the subject. "Is she your girlfriend? My *mam* seems to think she is, but all Henry said was that you were her neighbor."

"It's complicated." Sam scuffed his boot in the grass. "Henny's not exactly my girlfriend. I mean, she is to me, but... Well..." He squirmed the way he had back in their school days when their teacher asked him a math question to which he didn't know the answer. "She's just not there yet."

"So you're not *just* giving her a ride to and from work every day?" Chandler asked.

"*Nay*, I'm courting her. She's not calling it that yet, is all. Eventually, she'll see that it makes perfect sense. It's time she wed. Time we both did. Henn will come around. My plan is to have the banns called this fall. I'll be a married man by Christmas."

Chandler nodded, feeling disappointed for some reason and not knowing why.

Who was he kidding?

He knew *exactly* why. Because for the first

time in years, he was attracted to a woman. He was attracted to Henry.

When he first left Delaware, he'd dated a bit, but none of the women were the kind he'd marry. It hadn't taken him long to realize that many of his beliefs were based on his religious upbringing. No matter how hard he tried, he couldn't have the relationships with women that his *English* buddies had, and he'd resigned himself to the possibility that he might never marry and have a family.

At first, his friends had badgered him about being too uptight and not dating. Then they'd tried to set him up on dates with their girlfriend's sister or friend. But eventually, when he refused to go against his idea of what belonged outside a marriage and what belonged inside one, they'd given up on him. Now, on a good day, they called him *Bachelor*. On a bad day, it was *Preacher* or even *Bishop*. Their teasing had hurt his feelings, but he'd never let on because what was the point? Most of them hadn't been raised the way he had. They didn't understand respect for a woman or for marriage the way he did.

His mind flitted back to Henry. If he were honest with himself, he'd been attracted to her since he'd seen her dangling from his mother's roof. As he'd hurried across the yard, for the briefest moment, he'd imagined taking her out on a date in his truck or maybe just walking down to the pond on the family farm, holding hands with her. But Henry was Amish and he wasn't, and she lived here and he didn't, so he'd pushed those thoughts of her aside. Now they crept back into his head, and he felt guilty for thinking about her that way. He couldn't do that to Sam. Sam had been a good friend to him for many years back in the day, when Chandler was Amish. And the fact that his childhood friend had welcomed him had touched Chandler's heart.

Chandler shifted his attention to the volleyball match again. Henry's serve had been good, but the other young women in dresses and bare feet had managed to return it. The white ball went back and forth over the net as he tried to stop thinking about Henry. He couldn't. Turning to Sam, he narrowed his gaze. "So, let me get this straight. You think you're courting Henry, but she says you're not. What does she say when you ask her why she doesn't want to court you?"

Sam broke eye contact. "We haven't exactly talked about that. But it'll all come together," he added enthusiastically. "You'll see. I've got it all figured out. She's a nice girl, and her place is right down the road from ours. *Dat* has ten acres set aside for when I marry, and I've been saving for years to build my own house. Henny and I might have to live with my folks for a year or two, like Enos and Mary Aaron did, but girls don't usually mind that. My *mam* says it makes it easier, leaving their folks."

Chandler didn't know how to respond to any of that because it sounded like Sam was more wrapped up in the idea of getting married than wanting to marry Henry. Maybe he was wrong, but Sam and Henry didn't seem like a good match. Sam was a nice guy, but he was very traditional. And Henry wasn't. How would they make that work in a marriage? He wanted to ask but wasn't sure it was his place.

He was saved from saying something dumb when cheers broke out on the sidelines and Sam began to clap enthusiastically. The game was over, and Henry's team had won. Chandler watched Henry as she approached them, a smile on her face. This evening, she wore a blue dress that made her eyes seem bluer in the fading light. Her face was flushed from the exercise and loose tendrils of light red hair made her even prettier.

"Nice serving," Chandler said when she reached them.

She smiled up at him. *"Danki."*

"Water?" He pulled a bottle out of the back

pocket of his jeans. He'd grabbed it for her when he'd gotten the sodas for Sam and himself.

"*Ya*. I'm parched."

She smiled again at him as she accepted the bottle, and Chandler felt a weird sensation in the pit of his stomach.

"You best find your shoes, Henny," Sam urged. "You're going to get cold now that the sun's gone down."

"Thanks, *Dat*, but I'm fine." She wiggled her toes in the grass and took a drink of water.

The joke seemed to go right over Sam's head, but Chandler grinned. This was a different side of Henry than he'd seen when they'd worked together the previous day. He'd enjoyed her company as they worked side by side, but she'd been all business. He understood why, but he liked this Henry, competitive and funny. Really liked.

"Sam!" someone called from behind them.

They all turned to see Sam's brother standing in the distance beside the lean-to shed where they'd gather for the song and snacks. "Can you give me a hand?" Enos, who was two years older than Sam, waved at him.

"Coming!" Sam waved back and turned to Chandler. "Can you help Henny find her sneakers, and I'll meet you there?"

"Sure," Chandler agreed. When Sam walked away, he looked at her. "You need help finding your shoes, do you?"

They both laughed.

"They're right over there." She pointed toward the far side of the sand court and started to walk that way.

Chandler walked beside her. "Sam calls you *Henny*, short for *Henrietta*, I'm guessing. But you don't seem like a Henny to me."

She frowned. "I've asked him not to call me that, but—" She raised her shoulder and let it fall. "I guess he doesn't like *Henry*. A lot of people don't. It's a man's name and not fitting," she said.

"According to who?" he asked.

She walked slowly, seeming to enjoy the feel of her bare feet on the grass. The pleasure on her face made him want to pull off his work boots and socks and walk barefoot, too.

"Let's see, according to my aunt Judy and my uncle the bishop. According to half our church district…and Mary Agnes at the pretzel stand at Spence's Bazaar."

"Wait. Spence's still has a pretzel stand?" Chandler asked with surprise. He loved hot, freshly baked pretzels, and no matter how many times he tried them elsewhere, they never seemed to taste as good as the ones he remembered from Spence's. He dreamed about eating those pretzels.

They had reached her black sneakers, and she picked them up, still drinking from the water bottle. "They do, and they're my favorite. I like mine with—"

"Mustard," they said simultaneously, laughing.

"My sister Willa thinks mustard on pretzels is gross," she told him, her blue eyes twinkling with mischief.

"So Willa doesn't haven't to have mustard on hers," he returned. He almost said, "When we go for them," but he kept that to himself. He liked the idea of going to the Amish market for homemade pretzels with Henry, but it didn't seem right to suggest it. Not with Sam wanting to marry her.

"Oh, it gets better." She slipped one bare foot into a sneaker. "They also have pretzels stuffed with ham and cheese," she told him. "Like a hot pretzel sandwich. I get lots of mustard and dip with every bite. And they have hot dogs wrapped in pretzels, too."

His eyes widened with delight. "No way."

"You have to try them while you're here."

"Henny! Chandler! Come on! We're about to start!" Sam called to them from across the field.

Henry and Chandler both looked in Sam's

direction. "Guess we best go before we're in trouble," she said and started to walk. Then over her shoulder added, "Next time I go to Spence's, I'll get you a pretzel."

Her simple kindness so touched Chandler that he felt a sudden tightness in his chest. Then he realized that his boring, simple life had just gotten complicated.

After dropping Chandler off at his mother's house, Sam and Henry headed for their homes in Honeycomb. Sam was quiet except for the sound of him sucking a piece of hard candy, which was fine because she had a lot going on in her head. She found the sounds of the night insects, the rhythmic hoof beats and the rumble of the buggy wheels soothing, and she began to relax, letting her mind take her thoughts where they would.

She hadn't been happy that Sam had invited Chandler to go with them tonight. She hadn't even been happy about going to the singing at Enos and Mary Aaron's house at all. She didn't love events centered around socializing; she preferred to stay home and repair a fence or build a new nesting box for the henhouse. In the past, she'd always avoided singings and other events specifically meant for young men and women to mingle. She didn't appreciate the forced environment where women were on display for men to ask to give them rides home in their buggies. Up until a few months ago, she'd only gone to singings when she was expected to chaperone her eighteen-year-old sister or one of her sisters badgered her into attending. Then she'd started occasionally going with Sam, at her sisters' insistence. She went mostly because it was easier than listening to them talk for the next week about why she *should* have gone. About how she wasn't doing her duty to find a husband. It wasn't that she ever had a terrible time, but she never had a good time, either.

Until tonight.

This evening, she'd enjoyed herself. Playing volleyball for the first time this year had been nice, but she'd even appreciated the singing. It had been a fun evening, and she wasn't even sure why. What had been different, other than that Chandler had been there, which made no sense? It had just felt…right.

She looked up into the cloudless, dark sky, pinpricked with twinkling stars, and a strange feeling came over her. She had never been someone who heard *Gott*'s voice, but she often sensed His presence. Suddenly, she felt as if he was nudging her in some direction. Was that possible?

Before she had left home that evening, as she

was dressing, she'd sent a little prayer heaven-ward, asking God to guide her. She had meant concerning Sam and whether she should move forward with their relationship, but this gentle prodding she felt wasn't about Sam. It was about Chandler. And the longer she sat there, the stronger she felt it. Edee wanted to keep Chandler home so that she could help him realize he belonged there among their people. And Henry realized then that she was meant to help her friend. Help Chandler find his way because he was clearly lost.

Unable to keep her thoughts to herself, she turned to Sam.

"Sam."

"Henny."

They spoke each other's names over top of each other, then said, "I need to talk to you." They laughed nervously.

Sam nodded. "You go first."

"*Nay*, you first," Henry insisted, feeling an odd sense of nervous excitement.

He took a deep breath. Then another, and she felt bad that he was so nervous. She wondered how they could have been seeing each other for months and he still felt uncomfortable talking to her about anything serious. She also felt bad because she knew what he wanted to talk about, and he wouldn't like what she had to say.

He inhaled, switching the reins from one hand to another. "Chandler and I were talking about you tonight and—"

"About me?" She was surprised and oddly pleased. Then, she quickly said, "Sorry. I shouldn't have interrupted, Sam. Go on."

"He asked me if you were my girl, and I know you said you weren't ready to say you were, but I was wondering... Wondering—"

"—if I was ready now," she finished for him when he couldn't.

He nodded without looking at her. He gulped and reached into his pocket for another hard candy.

She studied him for a moment. She didn't want to hurt his feelings, and she didn't want to close any door that shouldn't be shut, but she knew she wasn't ready. The problem was that she wasn't sure how to explain to him that she was trying to see their relationship changing, going in that direction, but right now, the idea of courting him wasn't something she was sure would ever happen. She couldn't imagine marrying Sam.

Guilt settled in her chest. There was nothing wrong with Sam. Why didn't she like him the way he liked her?

She closed her eyes, thinking of what Eleanor had said that afternoon. Ellie had told Henry in no uncertain terms that it was time to put her childishness aside and grow up. She said it was time she, as a woman of faith, moved into the role God had set out for her. It was time to find a husband, and she thought Sam would be an appropriate choice. She'd praised his virtues for five minutes before their father interrupted them when he walked into the kitchen carrying four newly hatched Rhode Island Red chicks in a Bundt cake pan. While Eleanor sorted him out, Henry had escaped to the barn to clean stalls.

But there was no escaping now. She had to be honest with Sam. He was such a good man, and he deserved that honesty. She glanced at him, then focused straight ahead on the dapple-gray gelding's ears, which she could see by the headlights on the buggy. "I'm sorry, Sam, but—"

"But you're not ready. That's *oll recht*," he added quickly. "I understand. You need more time."

She squeezed her eyes shut, then opened them. "Sam, I'm not sure I'll ever—" She went quiet momentarily, then turned to face him. "Sam, I know you're eager to settle down to have a family." She hesitated and then went on. "So maybe you should start taking other girls home from singings. Annie told me tonight that Trudy Swartzentruber would give anything to have you ask her to ride home with you. And other girls feel the same way."

He was quiet as he unwrapped his candy, and again she heard the roll of the buggy wheels and the insects...and her heart thumping in her chest.

"Are you saying...are you saying you don't want me to...to let me take you to Edee's anymore? That you won't go to any more singings with me?"

"*Nay*, I'm not saying that. I'm just saying that, in the end, this may not go how you want it to. Between you and me. So...it's okay with me if you move on."

He was quiet long enough that she feared she'd been too straightforward. That she had hurt him with her honesty. But then he turned to her as he popped the candy into his mouth. "I thank you for that, but if it's *oll recht* with you, I think I'll make that decision myself. When the time comes. If it comes." He smiled at her. "Now what did you want to tell me?"

She wondered if she should push harder, but she was so proud of him for speaking up for himself that she let it drop. Besides, he'd be pleased with what she had to say. "I wanted to talk to you about Chandler."

"What about him, Henny?"

"It's *Henry*," she corrected, raising her voice.

She checked herself and went on, quieter this time. "Or *Henrietta* if you must, but please not *Henny*. Not anymore, Sam. I don't like it, and I've told you that. Several times."

When she glanced at him, he stared at her, seeming unsure what to say.

"You can call me either one. Both if you like, but I don't like *Henny*," she repeated firmly.

"Oll recht."

He drew out the words as if he had no idea what she was talking about, which annoyed her further. "All right," she repeated. "So, about Chandler. His mother wants him to stay in Rose Valley and not return to Illinois. She wants him to be baptized. To marry and give her grandchildren."

"Of course she does," he said. He pulled back on the reins, and the buggy rolled to a stop at an intersection. He looked at her, clicking the candy against his teeth. "She should. We all should. Because he belongs here," he declared with surprising fervor.

"Exactly. And I want to help Edee. I want to help Chandler realize that." Bright lights filled the buggy, and Henry looked into the rearview mirror. "There's a car behind us, Sam."

He gave his horse rein, and they made a left at the intersection. "So how do we do it? How do we keep him here?"

"I don't know exactly," she admitted. "I guess we need to make him see that he belongs here. We need to spend time with him. We need to make him feel welcome, a part of the community."

"Recht," he agreed. "We need to remind him of all the bad things in that *English* world."

Henry frowned. "I think that might be a mistake. We shouldn't tell him what's wrong with the *English* world. We should show him how good our world is. Remind him that there's still a place for him here. You know, he hasn't said this, but I get the feeling that he doesn't think he…he deserves to be here."

Sam offered a lopsided grin. "I think you're right. I'll pitch in, but besides his mother, you're the one who will spend the most time with him. I think you're the one who can do this if anyone can."

"Nay," she said quietly, looking at the bright stars. "It's not up to me, Sam. Ultimately, it's up to Chandler and *Gott*."

Chapter Six

Henry pushed back the lush green leaves of the strawberry plant and plucked a fat, red berry. "I'm serious, Annie. You couldn't have come at a better time," she told her friend as she dropped the fruit into a basket. "I don't know if I could have ridden all the way home with Sam today, listening to him crunch on his snacks."

Her friend Annie Lapp had surprised Henry by stopping at Edee's on her way home from Dover and offering a ride back to Honeycomb. Annie and Henry's sister Millie had been good friends for years. However, when Millie started dating Elden and had less time for friends, Henry and Annie struck up a friendship. Annie was the opposite of Henry, which was surprisingly one of the reasons Henry adored her. Annie was all girl and made no excuses for it. She had an entire closet full of dresses in every color permitted by their Old Order Amish church. She loved cooking and cleaning and had been running her family's household since she was sixteen, when her mother passed. As the only girl in a family of four boys, her father gave her complete control of their home, including the budget, and never expected her to clean horse stalls or bale hay.

Annie dropped to a seated position between the two raised beds and popped a strawberry, stem and all, into her mouth. "He doesn't really eat chips every day on the way home, does he?"

Henry added another strawberry to her basket. It was early in the season, and the berries were just beginning to ripen, but Eleanor had asked them to pick while they visited with each other so that no fruit went to the birds. "He does. Let's see…" She ticked off a list. "He eats potato chips, corn chips, cheese doodles, pork rinds, veggie sticks, pretzels. You name it. He's eating when he stops to pick me up at Edee's and still eating when he drops me off at the end of my lane."

Annie giggled, her green eyes dancing. She was a pretty woman, twenty-three years old with dark hair and cheeks that were always pink, except when they turned red when she was embarrassed.

"But not *every* time you're in his buggy with him?" Annie took a strawberry from her basket and ate it.

"Every afternoon," Henry replied, adding two more berries to her growing collection. When she and Annie had walked out into the garden, she hadn't thought there would be many berries to harvest, but she was pleasantly surprised to find that she was wrong. There were plenty of ripe ones, and there'd be more in another week.

Annie scooched closer to the garden bed. "But not mornings when he takes you to Edee's? He doesn't eat pork rinds in the morning, does he?"

"He does not. At least not yet." Henry spotted two fat strawberries and plucked them both from a plant. "*Nay*, in the morning, he eats doughnuts."

"Ohhhh, doughnuts." Annie grinned. "Homemade or store-bought? I do love a doughnut."

"Either. Both. But not just doughnuts, Annie. Little Debbie cakes, Pop-Tarts, iced buns, Tastykake Krimpets, even those yucky peach pie things you can get at the dollar store, two for ninety-nine cents."

Annie shrugged. "So he has a healthy appetite. He works hard, Henry. A man needs sustenance. And he's certainly not chubby like some of us." She patted her well-padded abdomen.

Her size was why she and Millie had become friends in the first place. Back in their school days, they were rarely invited to play softball or volleyball during recess because they were bigger than their other schoolmates. Which turned out fine for them because neither liked sports anyway. Instead, Annie and Millie had spent their recess taking walks together while dreaming of their futures with handsome husbands and lots of children.

Henry rolled her eyes as she added a handful of berries to her basket. "*Oll recht*, Sam needs the nourishment. He does work hard at his job and on his family's farm. But is it necessary to eat every minute he's alone with me?" She shook her head as she dug through the leaves. "He says he wants to court me. That's not my idea of courting, him talking between bites."

Annie's eyes got wide with excitement. "He asked you to walk out with him?" She smiled slyly. "Millie and I figured you were already courting and hadn't said so." She clapped her hands together. "That's so exciting."

"We are *not* courting." Henry eyed her friend. "He's been asking for weeks. I told him I'm not ready."

"Wait." She grabbed Henry's arm. "Sam Yoder asked you to walk out with him, and you said no? Henry, he is so nice, and he has a good job and… And his *dat* is going to give him land when he marries. He's a catch."

Henry frowned. "You think so? Then you marry him."

A full minute passed before Annie sighed and said, "Oh, dear-de-do. Not a good match, the two of you?"

Henry picked faster. "I don't know." Suddenly she was exasperated with herself and everyone around her who was sure Sam was the man she should marry. "How am I supposed to know, Annie? I've never done this before. Looked for a husband."

"What's wrong with him?" Annie crawled across the straw in the aisle to prevent weeds from growing and began to pick beside Henry.

Henry groaned. "There's nothing *wrong* with him. He's very sweet. I just… He…" She turned to look at her friend. "He's dull."

"But maybe he's shy with you, still because he adores you and he wants to marry you."

"That's just it. When Millie and Elden went out that first time, she was head over heels for him. She never thought he was boring."

"She was head over heels for him *before* they went out," Annie contradicted.

Henry threw a strawberry at her that had been half eaten by an insect, but her friend just laughed.

"You know what I'm trying to say, Annie. From that day at the school picnic when he bought her dessert, she knew she wanted to marry him. Even if he didn't think it would happen, she wanted it to. And I don't think it was long before he felt the same way. The same went for Beth and Jack."

"Not the same situation." Annie rose to her knees to reach farther. "They weren't all that friendly when he started building the store. Remember? It was right after he and Willa broke up. Beth was so angry at him because she thought he cheated on Willa. If I recall right, she wanted Eleanor to fire him."

Henry gave a wave of dismissal. "That's just how Beth is. She thought she was taking up for her sister, is all. The two of them were holding hands within weeks whenever they thought we weren't looking. And what about Cora and Tobit? Now there's a perfect match. The two of them are as alike as two peas in a pod. Both teachers. Both are as stubborn as Judy Troyer's mule. And they're as smitten with each other as I've ever seen."

Annie smiled dreamily. "So romantic. I think Cora and Tobit are going to marry, don't you? I think he's going to ask her any day now. Millie says they're together all the time, her helping him with grading his school papers. Him and his boy over to supper at your place at least once a week."

Henry sat back on her heels, suddenly tired from her long day. She and Chandler had spent hours fixing the hole in his mother's ceiling they'd had to cut to be sure no water pipes were leaking. Then they'd begun the tedious task of patching every hole in the walls. If she'd climbed the stepladder once today, she'd climbed it a hundred times. The work had gone well, and she and Chandler had easily found a rhythm to working side by side, but it still made for a long day.

Henry sighed. "Maybe I'm being foolish, Annie. Maybe I'm overthinking this, but is it terrible to want to feel my heart flutter when a man who wants to marry me walks into the room? I know those silly romance novels we used to buy from the book table at Spence's Bazaar weren't really true, but watching my sisters fall in love?" She lifted her gaze to meet her friend's. "I think the feelings described in those books are real. I hope they are." She dropped her hands to her lap. "But then I wonder if maybe that will never happen for me because of how I am. I'm not the kind of woman Amish men want to marry. I'm never going to be girly enough. Maybe the best I can hope for is to find a nice, hardworking husband who will tolerate me wanting to fix a leaky faucet once in a while and will make a good father."

Annie met Henry's gaze as she reached out to squeeze her hand. "You need to break up with Sam."

"What? But you just said—" Henry pressed her hand to her forehead. "I'm not dating him, so there's nothing to break up. I was very clear—"

"*Whatever* you're doing, you need to stop," Annie interrupted. Her face had grown serious. "He's not the right one for you, Henry. You're not falling in love with him. That's what those flutters we read about are. Love. Millie told me. They are real. You deserve to love, and Sam deserves to be loved. We all do. I can tell you I won't settle for a nice man with a good job. I also want my heart to flutter, and I won't stop looking until I find him."

Henry thought on that for a moment. "You don't think I'm being foolish? Or difficult? Eleanor is encouraging me to walk out with Sam. I'm only twenty-one. I don't know why she's being pushy about getting married. Willa's three years older than I am, and she's not wed."

"But not for want of trying," Annie quipped. "How many times have we thought she'd found the man she would marry, only for it to fall apart over one thing or another?"

Henry laughed, wiped the sand off a huge strawberry and took a bite. It tasted as good as it smelled. "Poor Willa. Every unmarried man from fifteen to fifty years old in the county seems to want to walk out with her, but it never works out."

"The right one hasn't come along yet, is all," Annie advised. "*Gott* has a husband for each of us. I truly believe that. We only have to be open to letting Him guide us."

Henry nibbled on her lower lip. "So you think *Gott* is leading me *not* to court Sam?"

Annie smiled kindly. "I don't know. Only you can know that. You have to listen to your heart and be open to the direction God nudges us. You know it's not always obvious what He wants for us. That's what my *mam* used to say. We have to listen carefully and quietly."

Henry drew up her knees beneath the skirt of her faded green dress. *"Nudge,"* she mused thoughtfully. "Funny you should use that word. On the ride home from Sam's brother's house last weekend, I think I felt a nudge from God."

"About Sam?"

"Nay. About Chandler, Edee's son."

Annie's eyes went round again, and she grabbed Henry's forearm. "*Gott* wants you to marry Chandler Gingerich? Henry, he is so handsome!"

Henry laughed and rolled her eyes. "No, God wasn't telling me to *marry* Chandler. Chandler's an *Englisher*. You know that. Everyone in the county knows it. At least, right now he is." She hesitated. She wasn't comfortable telling folks when she thought God spoke to her like others in their community. Because what if she was wrong? Worse, what if she justified her own wants by saying God was leading her? But Annie was a good listener, and Henry needed to talk about it with someone besides Sam. "That push I was feeling? It was to help Chandler find his way back to his faith."

Annie's brow furrowed. "You think you can make him become Amish again?"

"No one can make him, but maybe I can help him." Henry went back to picking. "I don't know if I can do anything to help, but I know it's what Edee wants. And I'm not sure Chandler likes being *English* as much as he thought he was going to," she said slowly. "We've talked a lot this week while we worked, and he doesn't seem all that happy. I get the idea he doesn't fit in as well with them as he had hoped."

"Wouldn't that be a wonderful thing, then?" Annie exclaimed. "To bring him back to our church and marry him?"

Henry laughed at the ridiculousness of her friend's statement.

"So what will you do to help him find his way?" Annie pressed. "I guess you can talk with him about our faith, but you have to draw him back into the community, too. So much of our life is about our friendships."

"That's what I was thinking. I thought I could invite him to fun activities to remind him what it feels like to be Amish. We've got that barn raising coming up, and…would it be weird to invite him to come to our place on a visiting Sunday? And Edee, of course. Or maybe I should invite him and his mother to supper."

"Who are we inviting to supper?"

Henry looked up, startled to see Eleanor standing at the garden's edge. She and Annie had been so engrossed in their conversation that they hadn't heard her approach.

"Um…" Henry sat back on her heels. "We were talking about Chandler and how Edee wants him to stay and eventually be baptized. And I'm hoping I can help. You know, because we're working together. So I thought I could invite him and Edee to supper sometime this week. If that's okay," she added. Eleanor was so overwhelmed with caring for the household, their *dat*, and the family store, and now her dear friend Sara was so sick. Henry didn't like creating any more work for her.

Eleanor walked toward them. She was the oldest of the sisters at twenty-eight and had proclaimed herself an old maid already. Although she was smart and pretty and could run a household as well as anyone Henry knew, she was insistent that she would never marry because, as a child, she'd had her leg amputated below the knee. She moved as fast as any of the sisters, and no one would ever know she wore a prosthetic leg unless she told them. She wore regular shoes, and the prosthetic looked no different than her other leg beneath the skirts of her dresses, which she wore a bit longer than most to cover it. But Ellie was stubborn, and once she decided something, she stuck to it, even when all evidence suggested she was wrong.

"I think that's a wonderful idea," Eleanor said. "Saturday night?"

"That wouldn't be too much for you? I know you're going to dialysis with Sara, and then you're making meals for her and her family."

"I'm going tomorrow with her. My new schedule is Monday, Wednesday and Friday to go to dialysis with her. And I already made a lasagna to tuck into the fridge so her husband can put it in the oven and have it ready when she gets home. So Saturday night works to have the Gingeriches over," Eleanor said, seeming more congenial than she'd been lately. Maybe she felt guilty for giving Henry such a hard time about Sam.

"I'll invite them tomorrow. I'll ask Edee so

Chandler won't have a chance to say no before she accepts."

Eleanor planted her hands on her hips. She looked more like their mother every day, and that made Henry happy and sad at the same time. "You don't think Chandler will want to come?" she asked.

"I think he might be hesitant," Henry admitted. "You know, because he left and some families don't want men like him in their homes, *corrupting* them and leading them astray, trying to get them to move to Illinois."

Eleanor chuckled. "You know full well it was never that way in *Mam*'s home. She always said the farther afield one of God's lambs has strayed, the closer we should hold them to our bosom."

"Aggie was like that, wasn't she?" Annie said fondly. "My *mam* was the same. Remember that time Saul and Tizzy Yoder wanted one of the Hostetler boys expelled from school for fighting? Your *mam* and mine went to the school board, saying he needed to be there all the more, him having just lost his father."

"Our *mam* used to say the hardest to love are the ones who need it the most," Eleanor reflected, her eyes getting misty. She sniffed, pulled a handkerchief from her apron pocket and wiped her nose. She'd always encouraged the family to acknowledge their loss and not be afraid to shed a tear in their mother's memory. "It's settled, then. You invite Edee and Chandler for supper Saturday night. Sara wants to stop at Spence's Bazaar on the way home if she's feeling up to it. I'll get something at the meat market." She looked to Henry. "Should I invite Sam, too?"

"No," Annie and Henry answered at the same time.

Eleanor looked suspiciously at them. *"Oll recht,"* she said, drawing out the words. But she didn't ask them to explain, probably because at least once a week she and Henry argued about Eleanor being too nosy. "How's the strawberry picking going? I was thinking we'd have a shortcake for dessert if there were enough ripe berries, but I didn't want to make up the batter if there weren't. You know how *Dat* is about his dessert these days. He doesn't like to be disappointed."

"Plenty of strawberries," Henry said, starting to pick again. "We'll be right in with them."

"Right in," Annie echoed.

Then Henry met Annie's gaze, and they both giggled. Why, Henry didn't know. But suddenly, she was in an excellent mood.

Chandler gripped the leathers in both hands and guided the two-seater buggy off the road and into the Koffman family's lane. He hadn't wanted to come to supper in the buggy; it had been eight years since he'd driven one. But his mother had insisted. She'd refused to let him drive them in his pickup, even though she used drivers regularly. She kept saying that going grocery shopping or to a doctor's appointment was different from going to a neighbor's home to share a meal. Ultimately, he had given in, as he suspected she knew he would.

He'd been nervous about driving the buggy for the first time in years. Being on the road in a buggy late on a Friday afternoon was dangerous. People were driving their trucks, cars and minivans too fast, looking at their cell phones rather than paying attention to the road. He would never forgive himself if he got into an accident with his mother. His worry had been for nothing, though. He'd been surprised how his fingers had remembered how to harness the horse then drive the buggy, even when his brain hadn't. He'd been equally surprised by how good it had felt to roll down the road slowly, seeing the flowers on the budding trees, hearing the insects and birdcalls and smelling freshly mowed grass. A man missed those things when he drove fifty miles an hour in a pickup.

He'd slowly relaxed during the half hour it

took them to drive the five miles to Honeycomb, but suddenly he was nervous again. The temperature was cooling down as the sun slipped downward in the western sky, but his palms were damp. He flexed one hand and then the other, realizing that his grip was too tight on the leathers.

He worried he'd made a mistake in accepting Henry's invitation to supper with her family. He knew she'd only done it to be polite. After working with him all week, she didn't want him at her kitchen table. He'd told himself he'd agreed for his mother's sake because the pleasure on her face had been so obvious when Henry extended the invite. But the truth was that he'd made the decision selfishly. When she was packing up to go, talking about possibly stripping the hardwood floor once they removed the linoleum the following week, all he had been able to think about was how dull the weekend would be without her. Eating supper with her family would only leave one day to go without talking about the best way to tackle patching the floor or replacing the one window that the sill had rotted on.

"It's going to be fine," Chandler's mother said, patting his hand. "The Koffmans are nice folks. I liked Henry's mother, Aggie, a lot.

They're a welcoming family. No need for you to be all fidgety."

"I'm not fidgety," he said, flexing his fingers again as they drove past Koffman's Country Store. He'd heard all about the store Henry and her sisters had opened to supplement their family income when their father could no longer work, but seeing it in person, he was even more impressed. The white building was appropriately Plain for an Amish business and looked more like a house than a commercial building, with inviting rocking chairs on a wide front porch. Pink azaleas bloomed in freshly mulched flower beds surrounding the store, making it even more welcoming.

"It's just supper," his *mam* said. "And I can promise you the food will be *goot*. When the Koffman girls first opened the store, they sold mostly dry goods and bulk foods, but Henry told me that one of their best money-makers has become selling homemade food all packed to-go. Baked goods, casseroles, soups, stews, you name it."

He shifted on the buggy seat anxiously. He knew she was right. There wasn't any reason to feel awkward. How many times had he sat around a table in an Amish home and broken bread with family, friends and neighbors in the first eighteen years of his life? It was just supper.

It was the shirt that was making him uncomfortable, he thought as they drove along the tree line that looked to be only a few years old. He ran his hand over the green fabric of the homemade long-sleeve shirt. His mother had washed the two he had brought with him but left them wet in the washer, so he didn't have one when he had to put on a clean shirt to leave. When she realized what she'd done, she'd apologized and suggested he wear one of his old shirts that she'd packed away in a box when he left home eight years ago. He'd protested, asking her what the Koffmans would think, him wearing Amish clothes, but she'd assured him no one would notice.

He found the plastic tub of his old clothes under his bed: two pairs of work pants, several work shirts, and some nicer ones like the green one he was wearing now and his church clothes. Surprisingly, all looked as clean and pressed as they had the day he left them. The green shirt had felt comfortable enough when he dropped it over his head, but now he suddenly felt self-conscious driving up in a buggy, wearing an Amish man's clothes. He had no right to these things. He'd given up that right when he left home.

"There's Felty," his mother said, waving at

the sixty-year-old man standing on the porch steps of the white two-story farmhouse.

Felty waved back.

When they reached the barnyard, Felty had walked out to the hitching post near the old dairy barn. And Henry was with him.

Chandler suddenly wished he'd stayed home. He didn't belong here. He didn't like all the nostalgic feelings washing over him.

Henry caught the horse's halter and used a lead line to tie him up. *"Welkom,"* she greeted. "We're so glad you could join us. I hope you like pork tenderloin because our sister Jane has made one big enough to feed half the county."

"Thanks for having us." Chandler spoke casually, trying to cover his nervousness. "Sounds delicious."

Henry met his gaze as he jumped down to walk to the other side of the buggy to assist his mother. "Nice shirt," she said, her words meant only for him. Her green eyes twinkled with amusement. "Looks an awful lot like the same one my *dat*'s wearing."

For an instant, Chandler didn't know how to respond. Then she smiled and he relaxed, happy he'd come after all.

Chapter Seven

Henry had been nervous about having Chandler and Edee to supper, though why she didn't know. Her worries were quickly set to rest when within fifteen minutes of their arrival everyone was talking at once as if the two families were best friends rather than merely acquaintances. To Henry's delight, Edee was as animated as she had ever seen her. She told the five sisters present that she was tickled to be at a table with so many women, and they had all laughed about the men feeling like they needed to stick together at the far end of the table.

Henry's *dat* took an immediate liking to Chandler and chatted with him through the whole meal, ignoring his daughters for the most part. The men discussed the weather, the new planting season and what Henry had planned for Edee's new kitchen. At one point, Henry saw Chandler cutting the meat on her father's plate as if it was the most natural thing, and his kindness touched her heart.

Felty Koffman's Alzheimer's was unpredictable, which frustrated both him and his daughters. From one day to the next, they never knew if he'd be able to do simple chores or even brush his teeth. They also saw changes in his speech; sometimes he couldn't remember the words for simple objects. On bad days, he became withdrawn and even argumentative. Thankfully, he was having a good day and was happy to participate in the family meal.

After a hearty supper of pork tenderloin, homemade sauerkraut, macaroni and cheese, stewed squash and fresh buttermilk biscuits, they had strawberry cake Jane had made, served with vanilla ice cream. When Eleanor caught her attention, Henry was licking the last of the sweet confection off her spoon.

"*Ach*, Henry, I completely forgot." Her sister, who had gotten up from her chair to fetch more coffee, pressed her hand to her forehead. "Could you have a look at Lindy's left front hoof? Our driving mare," she explained to Edee. She looked back at Henry. "She was limping this afternoon on her way into the barn from the pasture. I tried to have a look, but she wasn't having it. I think she knows I'm not good at that sort of thing."

Henry patted her mouth with a cloth napkin. "*Ya*, but I should do it before it gets too dark." She rose from her chair. "Want to check on Lindy with me, *Dat*?"

Her father pushed a heaping spoon of ice cream into his mouth. "Still eatin'," he said between bites. "But Chandler'll help you out. He knows a thing or two about horses."

"I don't *need* help, *Dat*."

"It's fine. I'll go," Chandler said, scraping his plate for the last bite.

Henry stood there feeling awkward. "It's fine. We don't put our guests to work. At least, not on the first visit," she added, trying to lighten the conversation. "I asked *Dat* because he likes to check on the animals with me."

The more accurate explanation was that sometimes her father got his feelings hurt when he wasn't consulted on certain matters of day-to-day farm life. Henry and her sisters had recently held a family meeting to talk about their *dat* while he went to town with their brother-in-law Elden. They'd discussed his latest appointment with his neurologist and what they needed to do differently to better care for him. One topic that had come up was their tendency to overprotect him, especially Eleanor. As the head of the household, Ellie was so focused on keeping him safe that the other sisters thought she was treating him too much like a child. But then they'd realized they all did it, to some extent. They constantly told him he couldn't do things like unload hay bales or split firewood for fear he'd hurt himself. They'd stopped asking his sentiments to avoid him not understanding or being able to respond. But they agreed that they were isolating him from the life he had known by doing those things and agreed they would include him as they always had and adjust as necessary when there was a true risk of injury.

"I'd like to go with you. That is…if you don't mind," Chandler said, getting out of his chair. "I need to stretch my legs." He patted his stomach. "If I keep eating like this, I won't be able to get up a ladder by the time I go back to work."

Henry watched as he picked up not only his dessert plate and spoon, but hers too, and carried them to the sink. A pleasant surprise. That wasn't something she saw an Amish man often do. Certainly not an unmarried one.

"Be back in a few minutes, *Mam*," Chandler told his mother as he followed Henry out of the kitchen. "We can go whenever you're ready."

"Take your time," Edee called after him. "I'm not going anywhere until I help these girls *rett* up this kitchen. And Willa wants to show me the new quilt she's working on."

Henry was quiet as she and Chandler put on their jackets alone in the mudroom. As she slipped into hers, she noticed that he was not only wearing an Amish shirt, but his denim fabric jacket looked like hers. His ballcap advertising a drywall company was an interesting contrast; he looked neither fully Amish nor fully *English*. She cut her eyes at him as they walked across the barnyard in the last light of the day. "Is Walmart selling Amish clothes in the Midwest these days?" she teased.

He grinned sheepishly. "*Mam* didn't finish the wash, so I had no clean shirt. Then I couldn't find the jacket I brought with me." He stroked his chin. "I was sure I left it hanging in the mudroom, but it wasn't there when we got ready to come here. I didn't have time to look for it. *Mam* kept some of my clothes after I left. Strange, but it worked out."

She pressed her lips together to keep from smiling. His innocence was charming. Did he not realize that his mother didn't finish the laundry so he'd be forced to wear an Amish shirt? And she suspected Edee knew exactly where his red canvas jacket was, especially since she'd commented on its inappropriate color the previous day. Old Order Amish in Kent County never wore red.

Henry glanced at Chandler. She wanted to

tell him that the shirt and jacket looked good on him. Looked right. But she held her tongue because even though he had to know that the entire community, including her, wanted him to return to the fold, she didn't want to be pushy.

"I see that mischievous smile," he said. "And yes, it did cross my mind that my *mudder* might know where my jacket is. I'm not *doplich*," he said, using the Pennsylvania *Deitsch* word meaning dumb. "But I didn't want to give her a hard time about anything. She's really worried about her surgery Monday."

"*Recht*. For her cataract," Henry acknowledged. Edee had gone to the rescheduled appointment, and her doctor had set a date for an outpatient procedure that would restore sight to her bad eye.

"Good thing is that I'll be here to take care of her afterward."

"*Ya*, that's *goot*," Henry agreed. She slid open the barn door and walked inside. They were welcomed with the sweet smell of fresh timothy hay and a cacophony of neighs, moos, bleats and clucking.

"Nice barn," Chandler said.

"*Ya*, old but nice," she agreed as she turned on one of the camp lanterns that hung from posts and rafters throughout the barn. They had switched from kerosene lamps to battery powered ones after their father had accidentally knocked one over while trying to turn it off. Thankfully, it had fallen on the clean dirt floor, and Cora had been there to right it, but it had been a warning to them all. The new lanterns charged by a solar panel Jack had installed on the barn roof.

Chandler slid his hands into his jeans pockets. "Nice place, the house and the outbuildings. How long have you lived here?"

She smiled nostalgically as she dug in a wooden box for a hoof pick. When she found it, she dropped it into her apron pocket. "I was born here. We all were, except for Eleanor. *Mam* and *Dat* bought the place after she was born."

"I was born in the house where my *mam* lives, too. It's nice to be back in Kent County."

"You miss home? I mean, where you live now." She walked to Lindy's stall. "I'm going to take her outside to get a better look at the hoof. Maybe you could hold up the light for me?"

"Sure." He accepted the lantern she held out to him. "I can't say I miss where I'm living right now," he said, sounding thoughtful. "I share a trailer with two other guys. It's crazy all the time. Ray and Justin are okay, but let's say their lifestyle's different from mine."

She raised her eyebrows questioningly and

snapped a lead line onto the roan mare's halter. "Hey, girl," she said softly to the horse. "Heard you have a sore foot. Think I can have a look?" She stroked the mare's neck to soothe her, then led her out of the stall.

Though the sun had set, there was still more light outside than in the barn, and Henry guided the horse to a hitching post to secure her. "I don't know what that means. You don't fit in with them?" She looked at Chandler from across the mare's back.

He met her gaze, his handsome face pensive. "That's one way to explain it. They do things differently than I do. Believe different things, so we're not well matched for roomies. It's partly my fault. I wanted to fit in when I left Delaware. I did things I'm not proud of. I didn't like who I was becoming. They're not bad guys, my roommates. It's only that they—" He stopped and started again. "Let's say there's drinking, smoking, drugs and bad choices."

"You do those things?" She ran her hand down the lower forelimb of Lindy's right foot.

He shrugged. "I used to smoke cigarettes."

She moved to the left side of the mare. "How long ago did you quit?"

Chandler followed her and held up the lantern. "Let's see. About nine days ago."

Smiling to herself, she ran her hand down

the mare's right foreleg, speaking softly to her, telling her what a good girl she was, then lifted her hoof to have a look. "You mean you quit when you arrived at your mother's."

He laughed. "When I crossed the state line. But I've wanted to do it for a while. It's a terrible habit, and it's expensive, too." He leaned closer so she could get a better look at Lindy's hoof.

Henry noticed at once that he smelled good. He must have cleaned up before he came to supper. She studied the soft inner structure of the hoof, trying to concentrate on the horse rather than on Chandler's proximity. "Did you drink alcohol, too? Do drugs?" she asked. The moment she said it, she wished she hadn't. "I'm sorry. I should mind my own knitting."

He chuckled. "I kind of miss people nosing into my business. Nobody in Illinois asks me personal questions. No one cares enough to be nosy."

She was still bent over, looking at the hoof, but she glanced at him over her shoulder. He was kidding, but there was also a thread of honesty in his tone. Maybe sadness. She looked down again.

"To answer your question, I never did drugs, but I used to drink alcohol. Mostly beer. I didn't like the kind of person I was when I drank, so

I stopped." He moved a bit closer with the light as she gently popped out a tiny pebble lodged in the soft flesh of the frog. "I'm fourteen months sober."

"I think that was it, girl." Henry released the horse's hoof. "We'll have a look at it in the morning." As she unclipped the lead rope from the hitching rail, she glanced at Chandler.

She didn't know much about alcohol. She'd never tasted it and didn't want to. But that didn't mean she hadn't had the opportunity. Some of the young men in Honeycomb who were not yet baptized considered themselves in their *rumspringa* years, even though the "running around time" wasn't permitted in the county. They would buy beer and drive around in their buggies on Saturday nights, drinking and listening to loud music from contraband radios.

She thought about Chandler's use of the word *sober*. That suggested he'd had a problem. A man she knew in one of the other church districts had had a drinking problem for years and almost lost his entire family over it. His preacher and bishop had stepped in and gotten him help, and he had been sober for several years. It happened in Amish communities, the same as with *Englishers*. Not as often, but most Amish disliked talking about it.

"Do you miss it? The alcohol?" she asked, not knowing why she was being so bold.

He shrugged. "Most of the time, no, but sometimes…" He lowered the lantern so she couldn't see his face, and walked beside her back to the barn. "Booze can be a crutch and that's where I was. I thought it was making me feel better, but it wasn't. The funny thing about alcohol and cigarettes is that you still want them sometimes. You still think you need them to deal with things sometimes. Even when you know it's bad for you."

She thought on that a moment, then said, "Well, I'm glad you don't do that anymore." She walked to the stall and released the mare into it. "Hey, did your *mam* ask you about going to the barn raising here in Honeycomb? Half the county is coming. Saul and Dotty Hershberger lost their main barn to a lightning strike last fall while they were at the hospital with a little one. It's in two weeks. I guess you'll still be around, what with your *mam*'s surgery coming up."

He smirked. "*Ya*, I'll still be here. For the surgery and to finish the kitchen. And no, she didn't mention it, but I'd be willing to pitch in." He passed the lantern to her after she closed the stall gate. "Growing up, I always loved barn raisings. I got to see all my friends and eat all the great food."

She laughed. "I go for the food, too." She dropped the hoof pick into the box and hung the lantern where it belonged. "I'm hoping the men will let me work on the barn rather than sticking me in the kitchen or on drink duty. It would be nice to have you there. Willing to work with me. No one ever wants to work with a woman with her hammer so my brothers-in-law get stuck with me."

He tugged on the brim of his ballcap. "I'd be happy to work with you, Henry. You're good at what you do, and I'll tell that to anyone willing to listen."

She met his gaze, and they stood there looking at each other for a moment. Then she turned off the lantern, sinking them into velvety darkness. As they walked out of the barn, she got the feeling that something had changed between them in the last half hour. She didn't know what, but she was keen to find out.

Chandler walked out onto the porch with only the light from the kitchen windows to illuminate his way and breathed in the cool night air. After gazing into the quiet barnyard, he carried the glass of chocolate milk his mother had insisted she make for him before she turned in. She remembered that the drink made from milk from their cow, cocoa powder and cane sugar had always been one of his favorite desserts. She said it was a way to thank him for all he had done that week caring for her after her successful surgery.

Smiling, he settled into one of the rocking chairs and sipped the creamy drink. He had dreamed of his mother's chocolate milk over the years, and it was every bit as good as he remembered. Better. She had explained that the secret was in whisking the drink to keep the cocoa powder from clumping.

He took another sip of the milk and set the glass on a table between two rockers. He was tired, but the good kind of tired, the kind that made him proud of how he had spent his day. He and Henry had agreed to take a few days off for his mother's cataract surgery and recovery, but today they'd put in a full day's work. After they removed the linoleum, they had successfully stripped the entire kitchen pine floor, including the pantry. On Monday, they'd start applying fresh polyurethane.

Working with Henry after not having her around all week had been nice. The only time he'd seen her since the night they'd had supper with her family was when she'd stopped by with her sisters to check in on his *mam* on their way to Dover. He'd kept himself busy all week doing small jobs around the house while his mother rested, replacing rotten fence posts, building a new ladder for the hayloft and cleaning out the dryer. However, none of the tasks had been as satisfying as his work with Henry. As much as he had tried to ignore it, he had missed Henry, and he wasn't sure what to do with that knowledge.

Something had changed between them Saturday night, but he couldn't put his finger on what it was. Maybe it was how warmly her family had welcomed him and the sense of belonging he had felt when they had all bowed their heads in silent prayer before the meal. Or maybe it was how her father had talked to him, treating him like his son rather than a man who had abandoned his faith.

All of those were possibilities, but he suspected that it was during the time at her barn that the shift had taken place. He couldn't believe he had confessed to her that he'd once had a drinking problem. He didn't know why he'd told her, but saying the words out loud had made him feel better. Being able to tell her about his failing and her listening to him had created a bond, like a gossamer thread strung between them even when she was miles away. Each night since, after saying his prayers on his knees, he lay awake trying to replay everything she'd said to him since they met. He relived every smile she'd gifted him, every brush of her hand when she passed a tool to him.

The sound of buggy wheels coming up the driveway startled Chandler, and he tilted his head, trying to figure out who had come visiting at half past eight on a Friday night. His first thought was that it might be Henry, and he rose from the rocking chair. Then he recognized Sam's dapple-gray horse. Maybe Henry was with him, he thought eagerly—then he saw only one person in the buggy.

Chandler walked to the porch steps and watched Sam turn his rig around in the barnyard and roll up in front of the porch. "Sam," he greeted, trying not to feel disappointed. "What brings you to this neck of the woods?" he asked as his friend climbed down from his buggy. "I'd have thought you and Henry would be out tonight."

"Not for want of trying. She said she couldn't go out." Sam crossed his arms over his chest and leaned back against his buggy. "Something about helping her sisters clean the floors at the store. So I came to pick up my *mam*. She's been at a birthday supper for a widowed friend on Hazletteville Road. My brother dropped her off, and I'm on my way there now, so I can't stay long. Just wanted to check in on you. On your mother. Henry said the surgery went well."

Chandler slid his hands into his pockets, feeling guilty about the thoughts tumbling around in his mind about Henry. Sam was smitten with her, and he had no right to think about her so much. "Surgery went very well. She's feeling good. Excited about being able to get back to her needlepoint." He smiled, feeling blessed that God had provided capable surgeons like hers.

Sam nodded slowly. "Glad to hear it. We've been praying for her." He glanced away, then back at Chandler. "Henry tells me you'll be joining us for the Hershberger barn raising a week from Saturday."

"Not this Saturday but next?"

"The Hershbergers had to change the date. It's the last Saturday of the month now. Saul went with prefabricated trusses, and there was a delay with the order," Sam explained. "But you'll still be here, right? You're coming?"

Chandler surprised himself by not hesitating. When he first arrived, he'd often considered his return to Illinois, but he'd been so busy caring for his mother that it hadn't crossed his mind in days. "Sure. I'll still be here. I don't want to leave until my *mam*'s fully recovered." He slid his hands into his jeans pockets. "Been a long time since I attended a barn raising. I'm looking forward to it. So's my *mam*. She says you don't see them like you used to. People are putting up pole sheds instead. Cheaper, easier."

"Glad you're joining us. We can use all the carpenters we can get." Sam tugged on the brim of his straw hat. "Guess I best be going. My *mam* will fuss with me if I'm late." He climbed back into his buggy. "Hey, a bunch of us are getting together for a softball game Sunday afternoon. It's a visiting Sunday for us. If you feel like joining in, we start at three. Bring Edee, too. Weather is supposed to be good, so there will be plenty of single girls to visit with."

Chandler grinned, shaking his head. "You know I know what you're doing. All of you."

"Doing?" Sam took up the reins, looking puzzled.

"My *mam*, you, Henry, the whole Koffman family, Janey Yoder next door." He hooked his thumb in that direction. "You're ganging up on me, Sam. Trying to lure me with strudels and pretty women. Trying to bring me back."

Sam thought for a minute, then lifted the reins to urge his horse forward. "We care about you. That a bad thing, my friend?"

Chandler was still trying to decide his response as Sam and his buggy faded into the darkness at the end of the lane.

Chapter Eight

Henry walked into Edee's shaded backyard and set her lunch bag and water bottle on the picnic table, where Chandler was taking his midday break. He was reading a paperback, something she'd never seen at an Amish worksite. He lifted his chin to acknowledge her presence and bent his head to return to his book.

She slid onto the bench across from him. He was eating a peanut butter and strawberry jam sandwich he'd made for himself. Edee had offered to cook him a hot lunch before she went to visit a neighbor, but he'd refused. He insisted PB and J was his favorite, especially when it was strawberry jam his mother had made. Henry, however, suspected it was his way of giving Edee time to rest and heal.

Not that Edee was complying with his wishes. Almost two weeks post-surgery, she had no pain or irritation and was eager to return to her daily routine. She'd left half an hour earlier, perturbed with Chandler because she had gone to remove wet clothes from the washer, only to find that he had already hung them on the line. Seeing the two of them go nose to nose over a basket of wet clothes had been amusing, especially since he towered over his mother by nearly a foot. But it had also been touching to see to what lengths he was willing to go to be sure she recovered from her eye surgery.

Henry pulled out a thick slice of sourdough bread, made in the family's store kitchen, and a chunk of yellow cheese from her bag. She hadn't had time to pack a proper lunch that morning. Her father had sneaked from the house and tried to let the cows out to pasture but had forgotten which gate to open and which to leave closed. Henry had woken to the sight of her sister, Willa, still in her nightdress, standing at the edge of her bed, flapping her arms and begging for help. Willa didn't like animals, which their mother had always pointed out was most unusual for an Amish farm girl.

Henry and Charlie, Jack's little brother, had rounded up the cows safely, but it had taken a bite out of Henry's morning. She'd sent Sam on his way without her and drove one of the family buggies to Edee's. Going alone had been so nice that she'd concluded that the time was coming when she had to decide about Sam.

She couldn't keep stringing him along, even if he insisted he was okay with her not knowing what she wanted.

Henry pulled the bread from the wax paper she'd wrapped it in. Only then did she realize that it was stale. She wrinkled her nose and glanced at Chandler reading his book.

She hadn't asked him about his change of attire since his arrival in Delaware, but he seemed to have given in to his mother's wish that he wear Amish clothing while he was home. Either that or she'd hidden all of his *English* clothes. The thought made her smile. Today he wore denim pants and a short-sleeve blue shirt she had made, with leather suspenders. Only the ballcap secured on his blond head suggested he wasn't Amish. She took a bite of her cheddar cheese, trying not to think about how handsome he was with his square, dimpled chin, butter-yellow hair and Amish clothing.

Her mind drifted. Was he considering remaining in Rose Valley and returning to the church? He hadn't said so, and she hadn't asked, but she had observed subtle changes in him. On visiting Sunday, he'd joined a community softball game at Sam's house and came by buggy again rather than his truck. She'd also overheard him speaking Pennsylvania *Deitsch* to Amos Kemp, the oldest man in Honeycomb at ninety-seven. Hearing the words come from Chandler's mouth had given her goosebumps.

Against her will, her mind wandered to more dangerous territory. If Chandler were to be baptized and join the church, he'd be expected to marry sooner rather than later. According to her uncle, men who returned to their faith found it easier to transition when they had a wife and little ones to occupy them. She wondered if Chandler's mother and other women in Rose Valley would put their heads together to find him a wife, or if he would be encouraged to make the choice himself.

If he joined the church, any woman would be blessed to have him as a husband. He was smart and kind, and not only could he repair a hole in a plaster ceiling, but he knew how to hang clothes on a line. She wondered what it would be like to walk out with him, date him. It wasn't a far-fetched thought. They spent so much time together that she considered him a friend. A good friend. Didn't it make sense to marry a friend? Someone compatible. The thought of it made her warm and a bit dizzy. She cleared her throat, took another bite of the dry bread and said, "What are you reading?"

"Ah…a Zane Grey novel. It's called an American Western, and it's set in the 1800s." He shrugged. "Kind of an adventure story.

Horses and good guys and bad guys. I've read a bunch of them. You can get them for like fifty cents at yard sales. I guess no one reads books like this anymore."

"Except you," she said, tossing her meager lunch onto the wax paper.

"Not good?" he asked, looking at the discarded bread.

She frowned. "Stale. I'll give it to the chickens. I was running late this morning and didn't get a chance to pack much of a lunch."

"Want part of mine?" He pointed at the sandwich beside a serving of homemade bread and butter pickle slices.

She hesitated. The sandwich looked good. "Those pickles didn't touch the bread, did they?"

He laughed, took half the sandwich and pushed the plate across to her. "What? You don't like pickles?"

"Love them." She picked up her half and bit into it. It was as good as it looked. "Just don't like them with my PB and J."

He smiled at her.

"It's good," she said, chewing. "But you know what I really want?"

"What?"

"One of those hot, gooey soft pretzel ham-and-cheese sandwiches from Spence's Bazaar."

His green eyes lit up. "I've been meaning

to get one." He took another bite. "It's Friday. They're open." He raised and lowered his eyebrows rapidly. "We could go."

"Now?" she asked, trying not to giggle at the silly face he made. "In the middle of the workday?"

"At *lunchtime*, Henry. When else would you get lunch? If I recall, the pretzel stand only stays open until they've sold all the pretzels and the fresh dough is gone. Then they pack up and go home to Lancaster, Pennsylvania. A family owned it by the name of Kurtz, right? Do they still have it?"

"They still own it, though I think the children bought it from the parents," she told him, stalling for time. She was intrigued by the idea of cutting out of work early and going for pretzels. And tempted. She never did anything impulsive like that. "You'd leave work early?" she asked.

"If I go with the boss, I think it's okay. My boss who ate half my lunch," he teased. "And why not? We stopped at a good place. The kitchen is cleaned up. Nothing we need to do so *Mam* can cook all weekend."

Edee was now without cabinets in anticipation of receiving the new ones. However, Chandler had set up a table she could use as a countertop. They were hoping the new cabinets would be ready the following week.

"I don't know," Henry said slowly. "I've never left early on a workday." She looked down. "And I'd have to change back into my dress. I can't be seen wearing pants in public."

"Come on," he entreated. "You know you want to."

"*Ya*, I want to," she agreed. "But it's not necessary to respond to every impulse."

"But it would be fun," he sang. "Come on, Henry. Didn't you hear your uncle talk about finding joy in our lives on Sunday? That God wants us to be joyful. He's a bishop. We need to follow his advice."

She cut her eyes at him. "I didn't know you were listening. I didn't think anyone was. It was a visiting Sunday. He wasn't supposed to preach while we tried to enjoy our lunch."

"Come on. Let's go get pretzels." Chandler looked at her, making a pleading face. "You know you want to," he whispered.

"Fine," she said, throwing up her hand in surrender. "We'll play hooky and get pretzels." She warmed to the idea immediately and grinned. "And maybe a slushy."

"Yes!" He came off the bench, gathering his book and the plate. "You run inside and change. I can bring the truck around if you take this stuff inside."

Henry picked up her own things then accepted his. "We're taking your truck?"

"Sure. Why not? I haven't driven it since I got here, just started it a couple of times. It's probably not good to let it sit." He narrowed his gaze. "It'll be quicker. And I know very well you ride in cars."

She returned his gaze. "Your *mam* won't ride anywhere with you in your truck. I heard her tell you so."

He waved her off. "That's because she's trying to make a point. That I can live without it. Come on, Henry, it will be fun. Being Amish doesn't mean you can never have fun, right?"

She strode past him. "Did I say it did?"

"So you'll go with me in the truck?" he called after her, sounding boyish and charming.

"This one time," she warned as she made a beeline for the house.

"Yes!" he called after her, pumping his fist. "You're not going to regret this, Henrietta Koffman!"

"I doubt that," she mumbled, but then she smiled. Nothing this exciting had happened to her in a long time.

At one on a Friday afternoon, Spence's Bazaar and Auction was a beehive of activity, a cacophony of sounds. There were shoppers everywhere, young and old, Amish and *English*, but there was a sense of excitement in the air, which smelled of freshly baked bread, popcorn and spring. Here, Tuesdays, Fridays and Saturdays, folks from all over the county came to buy food from the Amish market in one building and peruse the aisles of tables of antiques, fresh vegetables and flowers, baked goods and yard-sale junk offered for sale in a second building. And in warm weather, like the spring day they were having, tables and booths were outside. The parking lot was so filled with cars, trucks, and horse-drawn buggies and wagons that Chandler had to park along the street in front of a doctor's office.

The Amish market was busy enough that Chandler went to purchase the pretzels after a disagreement over who was paying—he won—while Henry tried to secure a table in the dining area. She only had to hover a few minutes before a Mennonite woman with three children waved her over.

"We're about to go," the woman said with a smile. "Joey, pop out so someone else can have your seat," she instructed her little boy. The mother's homemade dress was similar to Henry's mauve one, only it had tiny flowers on it. On her head, she wore a bit of lace pinned to her hair, which was twisted neatly at the nape of her neck.

"Thank you," Henry said as she took one of the four chairs.

"We're headed home to finish school for the day," the woman explained as she gathered her children. "Enjoy your lunch."

Henry waved to the family as they took their leave. She couldn't remember the last time she'd sat down in Spence's eating area. Usually, she was too busy. She'd dash in, buy lunchmeat, fresh fish or a bag of soft pretzels and then be on her way. Seated there now, she remembered how much she had enjoyed sitting at the tables with her *mam* and sisters and people-watching. *Englishers* always wore such interesting clothes and she enjoyed hearing bits of their conversation.

She didn't have the opportunity to people-watch for long before Chandler arrived carrying two frozen slushies and a handled brown grocery bag. She jumped up to take the drinks from him. "Did you buy out the pretzel stand?" she asked, laughing at the size of the sack.

"No, but I didn't know when we'd get here again." He set down the bag and slid into a chair across from her. "My boss isn't much for taking time off for lunch."

"You most certainly do get time for lunch,"

she argued playfully as she unwrapped one of the straws. "Thanks for getting cola flavor."

"It's the best one." He grimaced. "I'm not one for blue or red drinks."

"Me either. My sisters Willa and Millie love the blue. They say it's blue raspberry, but no raspberry I've ever seen was blue." She sipped her frozen drink and watched eagerly. The delicious smell of freshly baked pretzels wafted from the bag.

"Let's see," he said, peering into a white lunch sack he'd pulled out. "Hot ham and cheese for you." He passed it to her and dug into the big bag again. "And for me. And I got a couple of hot-dog pretzels, in case we're still hungry." He set it down. "And for dessert, cinnamon-sugar pretzels." He set another small bag between them. "I got a couple more of the ham and cheese and some plain pretzels to take home. *Mam* likes pretzels, too." He tore open the bag in front of him to reveal his pretzel sandwich wrapped in foil. "Oh, and I got mustard." He fished out several plastic condiment cups with lids on them. "I didn't know what kind of mustard you like, yellow or spicy, so I got both."

She took one of the containers on the table between them. "I like yellow mustard, too, but spicy brown's best with ham." She put her hand into the bag he'd passed to her and pulled out two foil packets. "You got me *two* sandwiches?" She stared at him wide-eyed.

"Sure." He lifted one shoulder and let it fall. "I've seen you eat. You work hard, and you've got a healthy appetite." He took a big bite. Butter dripped from the corner of his mouth, and he grabbed a handful of napkins from the dispenser on the table. "I like a woman who isn't shy about eating. I once dated someone who would go out for supper with me and eat half a hamburger patty without the roll and like three French fries. Then she'd say she was stuffed." He shook his head. "No way that's how she eats every day. But she didn't even take the leftovers home."

"Have you dated a lot since you left Kent County?" she asked. Then she felt herself blush, and she looked down at the table. "I'm sorry. I shouldn't have asked. It's not my business."

"Ask anything you want," he told her. "The answer is no. I haven't dated much. Wanted to, but—" He hesitated. Then sighed. "I guess no one ever clicked. I learned quickly that I could dress *like the English guys*, but you can't change what's in here." He tapped his chest over his heart. "Not even if you think you want to."

"What do you mean?"

He wiped his mouth with a napkin before he

spoke. "I guess it comes down to what *English* folks call values. What you believe is right and what you think isn't. What's important to you, and what isn't. It's been hard for me to fit in and keep my values. Like I told you before, I've done stuff I wish I hadn't. And the thing is—" He met her gaze. "Doing them didn't help me fit in with the guys any better. They just made me feel more like an outsider. And like I wasn't being true to my—"

"Values," she finished for him.

He pointed at her. "Exactly."

She took a bite of her ham-and-cheese pretzel sandwich. It was every bit as good as she remembered. "Can I ask you something else?"

"Sure." He picked up his drink to take a sip.

"Even if it might make you angry?"

He smiled at her in a way that made her feel warm all over. "I could never be angry at you, Henry. At least, not for long," he added.

She smiled back at him then became serious. "If you don't fit in out there in the *English* world, Chandler, why don't you stay here?" With us, she wanted to say. With me. But she didn't say it aloud.

He sat back in his chair, setting the cup down without drinking. He didn't look at her as he responded. "I've been gone so long, Henry. I don't fit here anymore. I don't fit anywhere."

The tone of his voice sounded sad, which made her sad. "I don't think that's true," she told him. "I think with some time, you could fold right back into the fabric of the community."

"I don't deserve that," he said, his voice emotional. "I had my chance, and I gave it up. It's too late to come back."

She studied him. Most of the time, he was so upbeat and energetic, but now he looked like a bone-tired man at the end of a long workday that hadn't gone well. He looked defeated. She leaned closer to him. His hand was on the table, and she covered it with hers before she could stop herself. "It's never too late to come home, Chandler."

He shifted his gaze to their hands, and she pulled hers away. She grabbed her slushy and sipped noisily to cover her embarrassment. She had never once touched Sam that way. She wouldn't even let him hold her hand when they walked together, even though he'd wanted to. What was wrong with her? Why wasn't she attracted to him like she was Chandler? Sam was a good man and was baptized in the church, just as she was. He would be a good choice for a husband.

She and Chandler were quiet for several minutes as they ate. Then he started telling her a funny story about a jobsite he worked that was overrun with frogs. One of the guys he worked with complained so much about them that the other men, including Chandler, started putting them in the guy's toolbox, his pickup and even his lunch cooler. Soon she and Chandler were laughing, and the momentary black cloud over him evaporated. As he talked, he became more animated, and thoughts from earlier in the day crossed her mind again.

If Chandler joined the church, he would make a good husband for an Amish woman. He was kind and caring—which was evident in how he treated his mother. But he was also smart and a hard worker. And so talented. His construction skills were excellent, but he could also fix anything. He was like her in that he liked knowing how things worked. He could take something apart and put it back together, only better, making it whole again. And he was a good companion. He was a good conversationalist but also knew how to be quiet. He knew when to enjoy a moment in peace, whether they were sanding a floor or taking a lunch break in the backyard. Those were all attributes she wanted in a husband.

But he wasn't Amish.

She chastised herself silently. It was a waste of time to think about what kind of husband he would make for an Amish woman—for her—because he wasn't Amish, and so far, he hadn't said he wanted to be.

To Henry's surprise, she ate both sandwiches Chandler had brought her, though she passed on a hot dog. Then she started on a cinnamon-sugar pretzel, dipping it into the homemade caramel sauce he had bought to go with them. She was so engrossed in her conversation with him that it took her a second to realize someone had spoken her name. When she looked over, she saw Sam standing at the end of the table, a bag in one hand, a corn dog on a stick in the other.

Seeing him out of the blue startled her, and she drew back. "Sam." She swallowed her last bite. "What are you doing here?"

Sam glanced at Chandler, then back at her. "I was going to ask you the same question." He looked at his friend again. "Not trying to steal my girl, are you?" Then he laughed and returned his attention to Henry.

She and Chandler seemed to decide at the same time to ignore Sam's joke.

"We, um, I…" Uncomfortable, she wiped her mouth with the last napkin from the dispenser. Why did she feel like this? Like she'd done something wrong? She wasn't doing anything wrong; she was eating with her coworker. "We came in for lunch. I wanted pretzels. Why are you here and not at work?"

Sam took a bite of his corn dog and chewed loudly. "Rode into town with one of the Mennonite guys to get nails. We decided to stop for lunch." He held up his bag. "Two for the price of one on the corn dogs after one o'clock. Want one?" He offered the bag. "I got six, so there's plenty. Tater tots, too, with cheese and bacon."

She offered a quick smile. "No thanks." She glanced at Chandler and slid out of her chair. "Be right back. I'm going to find more napkins."

Chandler watched Henry go as Sam took a chair across from him.

"I was just jokin' about you taking my girl," Sam said with a chuckle. He pulled another corn dog from the bag. "I'm not even sure she is my girl. Or ever was." He took a bite, not seeming the least bit upset. "My *mam* says it's time to start looking at other options. She's decided we're not a good match, me and Henny. She thinks the Koffman girls are too wild, anyway. They don't know their place."

Chandler listened without speaking because he wasn't sure what to say. Henry certainly wasn't *wild*. None of the Koffman women were. Henry was a faithful woman. A godly woman.

Any man would be blessed to have her as his wife. But she *was* unconventional, and he had a feeling that Sam's mother, like many women in the Amish community, categorized women who had a mind of their own that way.

"What do you think?" Sam asked.

Chandler blinked, feeling like he'd missed something. "About what?"

Sam leaned back in his chair, talking between bites. "About me and Henny. Do you think we're a good match? Do you think she'd make a good wife for me?"

Chandler was startled by the question, and for a moment, he didn't know how to answer. Did he tell Sam what he wanted to hear? That she would make him a fine wife? But his friend's question wasn't if she would be a good partner in life to someone, it was if she was suited to him and him to her.

And it was wrong to lie.

Chandler cleared his throat. "You really want to know what I think?" he asked quietly.

Sam leaned back in his chair. "Of course. That's why I asked. Growing up, you always gave me good advice."

Chandler clasped his hands together on the table, almost as if in prayer, and looked down and then up. "No, Sam. I don't think you're a good match. I think your personalities—" He groaned, unsure what to say. How much. Because he didn't want to upset his friend. Sam had been good to him since he arrived, welcoming him, making him sometimes feel like maybe he could belong here.

Sam waited as Chandler tried to gather his thoughts.

"I think… I think a man and a woman ought to be compatible in day-to-day things, Sam," Chandler went on. "I believe you should think the same way or at least understand why others think the way they do. You should feel happier and more fulfilled together than apart. And… and I'm worried that if you and Henry marry, she'll—neither of you," he corrected himself quickly, "is going to be happy."

Sam nodded slowly, seeming to chew on the information as he chewed his lunch. "I think I get what you mean. Kind of what maybe she's been trying to tell me." He sat back in the chair. "But that means starting all over again, and I wanted to get married this fall."

Chandler leaned closer to his buddy. "You deserve to have a wife well suited to you. You're a nice-looking guy, a good guy with a good, steady job. I imagine half the single girls in the county are smitten with you, Sam."

"Smitten with me?" Sam grinned, his face reddening. "You think?"

His reaction surprised Chandler. But it shouldn't have. From the very beginning, he'd thought Sam was more enamored with the idea of marriage than the idea of marrying Henry.

"Got some!" Henry announced, walking back to the table holding up a stack of napkins. "Anna Kurtz at the pretzel stand knew where they were kept." She started loading the napkins into the dispenser. "We should get going, Chandler. There's one more thing I want to do in the kitchen before we take off for the weekend."

Sam rose to go, and Chandler breathed a sigh of relief.

Chandler couldn't have been happier to see Henry. While Sam didn't seem uncomfortable with the conversation, he certainly was because his buddy's earlier joke about him trying to steal his girl had hit home.

The truth was that he wished Henry *was* his girl.

Chapter Nine

Sunday, a visiting preacher, Ezekiel Mast, spoke on the Good Samaritan. Ezekiel came once a year to see his brother, Jim Mast, and always preached when he visited the family. Preacher Ezekiel had once again chosen the same message from the New Testament that he chose every year, and it was one he could speak on at great length. Henry knew the passages well and enjoyed his words for the first hour, but as the minutes ticked away, she began getting as antsy as the little Yoder girls on the bench in front of her.

She had sat beside her sisters Jane and Millie near an open window. As always, the women sat on long benches on one side of the aisle, the men on the other. Depending on whose home they met in, they were sometimes squeezed closer together, but Edna and Jim Mast, owners of a profitable orchard, had recently added an addition to their home large enough to be used for church or other community gatherings. Henry enjoyed services at the Masts' and liked that they'd put in so many large windows. She appreciated being able to gaze out at the apple and peach trees that were now bursting with blossoms as she listened to the words of *Gott*. She watched a fat gray robin with its orange underbelly alight on a branch. As it landed, petals from the white blossoms fell and scattered in the wind like snow.

Preacher Ezekiel's voice thundered out, echoing off the high white ceiling as he warmed to his subject and began to repeat himself for the third time. Henry tore her attention from the robin to focus on the man's words again. However, as her gaze swept the room, she spotted Chandler seated across the aisle. He wasn't watching the preacher, either. He was staring directly at her. And when their gazes met, he smiled at her.

Startled, Henry averted her eyes, but he was still watching her when she glanced back from under her lashes. Like the other men, he wore a white shirt, a black coat, vest and pants, and a black wide-brimmed hat. He looked quite handsome and as Amish as any man in the room. She looked away.

She supposed she should have felt disapproval. Chandler had come to services of his own free will and should have been concentrating on the sermon, but the truth was, she was secretly pleased. He sensed it, too, she thought. *He feels this invisible thread binding us together, drawing us closer.* When Preacher Ezekiel finally wrapped up his sermon, and the congregation rose to offer the final hymn, she stole another glance at Chandler and found him looking at her again instead of his hymn book.

Standing beside her, Millie elbowed her. "Henry," she whispered as voices raised in praise around them. "Pay attention." Her nut-brown eyes narrowed. "Why are you looking at Chandler?"

"I'm not *looking* at him," Henry whispered, bumping her back with her elbow.

"Well, he was looking at you." Millie smiled as she focused forward. "Good job getting him to come to service. And in a buggy, no less. I was afraid he would show up in that big truck and set our uncle into a tizzy. Bishops don't like motor vehicles at Sunday services."

Jane shushed them, and Millie and Henry suppressed a giggle and joined in on the chorus.

When the hymn ended, everyone sat down, and Bishop Cyrus offered a traditional prayer in High German before dismissing the congregation for the midday break. There would be a short service after the communal meal, consisting of prayers and a few more hymns, and everyone would leave by four o'clock.

When the service ended and families rose and gathered their children and belongings, Millie grabbed Henry's arm and pulled her aside. "Have you broken things off with Sam?"

Henry avoided her gaze. "Sam and I were never—"

"Enough with that," Millie chided, surprising Henry. Millie was never short-tempered with her. She was never short with anyone. "If you are still with Sam, if he *thinks* you're with him, then it's wrong for you to look at Chandler that way."

Henry folded her arms and stared at her black leather Sunday shoes. She was annoyed now. This was the problem of having so many sisters. They never knew when to mind their own knitting. "I don't know what you mean when you say *looking at him that way.*" She shrugged. "It's how I look at…people." When she glanced up, her big sister was gazing at her sternly.

"But he was looking at you, too," Millie murmured, blocking anyone's view of Henry.

Henry didn't know what to say. The previous two nights, she'd lain in bed long after the lights went out, going over in her mind her trip to Spence's with Chandler. From the moment he'd suggested playing hooky until they returned to Rose Valley in his pickup, windows down, sunshine on her face, the day had been perfect. One of the best she could remember in her adult life. Lying there, listening to Cora snore softly, she had turned over in her mind every smile, every bit of conversation and laughter between her and Chandler. Sam had joked about Chandler stealing his girl, but she couldn't help wondering if there was any truth behind the jest.

"Henry, are you listening to me?"

Henry focused on her sister's round, pretty face. Millie suddenly seemed older, more mature, like Eleanor or their mother. She had an air of authority about her that was unlike her. "If Sam is still under the assumption—"

"Do we have to talk about this right now?" Henry interrupted.

"It has to be said, and better coming from me than Eleanor. Or our aunt, Judy," she added. They both had many opinions on how the Koffman women should behave and never hesitated to express them. "If they saw the way you and Chandler were looking at each other—"

"We were not—"

"He's not one of us anymore," Millie reminded, speaking over Henry. "You need to think hard about what you're doing. If you were to fall in love with him, that would mean leaving Honeycomb. Leaving your life. Your church."

"I am not leaving here. Not ever," Henry responded firmly.

"*Goot.* But that means you need to be careful. A woman's heart can only be broken if she gives it away."

Henry stared at Millie.

"Guard your heart, *schweschter*," her sister warned. "That or convince him to be baptized and rejoin his community."

"Millie!" Jane called from the far side of the room. "Are you coming? Those cakes won't fall into slices on their own."

"Coming!" Millie called over her shoulder. She met Henry's gaze again. "It may be time you and Chandler have a conversation. But it would be best if you settled matters between you and Sam first. And soon, because if you two are looking at each other that way in front of Sam—" She pointed at Henry.

Henry grabbed her finger. *"Oll recht. Oll recht."*

"Sooner than later," Millie warned as she walked away.

Annoyed with her sister, Henry slipped through the door that led outside, following the men rather than the other women through the house to the kitchen. Because the weather was so nice, everyone would eat outside, where long tables had been set up for the traditional shared meal. The men would stand around outside and talk about the weather and crops while the women brought out the meal for the first seating, consisting of the men and guests. The women and children would eat afterward, partaking of the same food but with much less formality than the first round. With the men fed, the women would be free to visit and eat at their leisure.

Henry knew she would be expected to help serve the men with her sisters and the other women, but she needed a moment to herself. She had to think about what to do about what Millie had said. She needed to make sense of all the thoughts in her mind and feelings in her heart. Deciding that if she could be alone for a few minutes, she'd be all right, she slipped around the corner of the house, out of sight of the other churchgoers.

To her surprise, Chandler was standing right there, and she nearly bumped into him. She pressed her hand to her heart. "You...you startled me. What are you doing here?" she asked, gazing around. The men had all gone out into the barnyard. No one could see them where they were standing.

"Waiting for you," he said. He'd removed

his black coat due to the heat, and it hung over his arm.

She frowned. "How did you know I was coming out here?"

"Saw you through the window."

"So you're spying on me?" She covered her self-consciousness with a tone of annoyance.

He laughed. "Something like that, I suppose. I wanted to say hello. I was afraid I wouldn't get to talk to you. You know, me sitting with the men and all." He looked away, then back at her. "I've been invited to share the meal with your uncle."

"Ah, that's a seat of importance."

He glanced away with a smile. "He said he had a conversation with my mother this week and wants to talk. She didn't tell me she'd talked about me with him or about what."

"But you can guess," she said quietly, thinking again how handsome he was in his black-and-white Sunday clothes. She liked how his blond hair fell to his collar, contrasting with the dark wool hat.

"I can guess he wants to set up a meeting to discuss counseling and baptism classes. *Mam* brings it up half a dozen times a day."

Henry felt her heart skip in her chest. If he were to be baptized—she refused to think about it right now. "So…you're considering speaking with him."

"It's all my *mam*'s idea, of course."

"You didn't answer my question." She hesitated and then said, "Are you considering it?"

He groaned. "I don't know. Yes. No. Maybe." He met her gaze. He had the most beautiful blue eyes, so full of life.

"Well, which is it?" she asked. She thought about telling him that Millie had caught them looking at each other. That her sister had seen something between them, but she wasn't brave enough. Bringing it up might lead to a discussion of feelings, which scared her. Her growing feelings for him scared her.

Henry studied Chandler's expression. He was obviously undecided, and thoughts of herself faded. She softened her tone. "It's *oll recht*. You don't have to tell me anything. I shouldn't have asked. I need to get to the kitchen to help the others with the meal." She turned to go, but he grabbed her hand, and the warmth of it caught her off guard. But it felt right, the same way touching him had felt right the other day at Spence's.

Feeling Henry's warm, smaller hand in his made Chandler want to hold her hand forever. He had been telling himself for weeks that he liked her as a coworker and friend, but suddenly he realized—no, he *admitted* to himself that he was falling in love with her.

That realization, as she met his gaze, was exhilarating. Frightening, too. He'd never been in love. He hadn't been entirely sure love truly existed between a man and a woman. He had little recollection of his parents' relationship. He remembered them being comfortable together, and maybe they loved each other because of the life they had built together. But he had never seen them as being in love, like the kind of love he'd seen on TV and in movies. He'd thought that romantic love didn't exist among the Old Order Amish the way it did with *Englishers*. But maybe he believed that because he'd never known that there were Amish women like Henry until he returned home to Rose Valley.

One of the reasons he left the Old Order Amish in the first place was that he had never been able to see himself married to any of the docile young women he knew. He wanted a partner in a wife and one willing to share their family's responsibilities rather than placing all the weight on his shoulders. It was too much, he feared—working a construction job, running a farm and being responsible for the religious upbringing of children. But he was older now.

Wiser, he hoped. Unexpectedly, he could imagine himself married to an Amish woman like Henry. No, he could imagine being married to Henry. He could see a life on the farm he had grown up on with his *mam*. In his mind's eye, he could see a family of his own, children of his own…redheads who looked like their mother. Like Henry.

But that would mean returning to his faith.

Could he do that? Did he want to? He'd spent almost as much time over the last two days thinking on that matter as he had about Henry and their trip to Spence's on Friday. He had concluded that he wanted to return to the church but was afraid. He was afraid he would never be the man he needed to be as a member of the Old Order. In the *English* world, he hadn't lost faith in *Gott*; he'd lost faith in himself. Was that something Bishop Cyrus could help him with?

"Chandler," Henry whispered, looking at their hands still linked. "Someone will see us. Someone might tell Sam, and I wouldn't want to—"

"Sam asked me if I thought you two were a good match," he interrupted, releasing her hand.

"He did?" She stepped back and crossed her arms. "When?"

She wore the same Sunday clothing as the other women, all black: the dress, the triangular cape pinned to her back. Over her red hair was her starched white prayer *kapp*, symbolizing her faith, but she looked nothing like the other women. No one could hold a candle to her beauty.

Chandler's mouth felt dry, and even though he had removed his coat, he was suddenly hot. He tugged at the high collar of the pristine white shirt his mother had held for him for eight years. He wished he could also take off the black vest, but that would be inappropriate, and everyone had been so welcoming to him today that he didn't want to do anything that might offend someone. His gaze met Henry's. She was waiting for a response to her question.

"The other day at Spence's. He asked me what I thought about the two of you as a couple," he said quietly, wishing now that he hadn't brought up the matter.

"And what did you say?" she pressed, moving closer to him.

He took a breath. His heart was beating hard in his chest. He was in trouble here. He was in terrible trouble because he didn't know if he could live without Henry. But he didn't know if he could live the life he would need in order to be with her. "He's been my friend for a very long time. I had to tell him the truth."

She waited.

He swallowed. "I told him that I didn't think you two were compatible. That he was a good guy. That he'd make a good husband, but not for you." His last words came out in a whisper.

Henry's eyes had grown round. "You said that?" she whispered back.

He nodded, pressing his lips together to keep from proclaiming his love right there in someone's backyard on a church Sunday. "I had to be honest. He's been too good a friend not to be."

She crossed her arms. "And how did he take it?"

"Well," Chandler answered. He didn't want to tell her that Sam's mother didn't think they were well suited either, fearing it might hurt her feelings. There was no need to repeat that. "He didn't say so, but I got the feeling he's been thinking the same thing." He watched her lower her head and look at the grass as if she was upset by that, and, for a moment, he feared he'd made a terrible mistake. Had he imagined that Sam's girl liked him more than she liked Sam? "I'm sorry," he said. "I shouldn't have told you that."

She laughed, but it was without humor. "*Nay*, that's a good thing."

He hadn't realized he was holding his breath until he released it. "Is it?"

She nodded, not looking at him. "I'm relieved. Because you're right. You both are. Sam and I...we don't think the same way. He doesn't understand me. It's my fault. I knew that. It's only that my family—" She pressed her lips together. "They worry that no one will want me. Because of how I am." She hesitated. "And I do want to marry." She looked up at him, and he saw tears in her eyes. "But I can't be someone else to make another happy, not even my husband. Because *Gott* made me this way. Didn't He?"

It was all Chandler could do not to take her in his arms and hold her tight. He wanted to tell her that he thought she was perfect as she was and that he would take her for his wife and feel as if he was the most blessed man, *English* or Amish, to ever walk the earth. Instead, he held his hands to his sides and said, "God did make you as you are. And Sam as he is. And Henry, I don't think you'll have a hard time finding someone to marry you. I think the right person hasn't asked you to walk out with them yet, is all."

She looked at him and smiled the sweetest smile. "Really?"

They held each other's gazes, and he was certain that she felt the same connection to him that he felt to her. He was so sure that suddenly he became bold. Or foolish, because he said, "I'd fancy walking out with you. If I were to stay."

She pressed her hand to her mouth but didn't break eye contact. "Millie caught us looking at each other. In service. And…she thinks—I think I need to break things off entirely with Sam."

"I agree," Chandler said, almost feeling as if he were in a dream. "If he's not right for you, it's not right to make him think there's still a chance things could work out between you."

She nodded. "I'll have to wait a few days. Yesterday, he stopped at our family store. I was putting in some more shelves in the kitchen. He came to tell me that he was working a job in Rehoboth Beach this coming week and the days would be long because of the distance. One of the crew's Mennonite guys will pick him up at his house each morning and drop him off, so we won't be riding together all week. He plans to be at the Hershbergers' barn raising Saturday, though. I could talk to him them." She looked at him as if seeking his approval.

He nodded slowly.

"But this week, you need to think hard on

what you said," she continued. "What I think you're saying. About you and me. *Oll recht?*"

"Oll recht," he repeated. Then he grinned at her.

She smiled back. "I best get to the kitchen to help with the meal before one of my sisters comes looking for me."

Chandler stepped out of her way to let her pass, his gaze on her until she disappeared around the side of the house. As he watched her go, it occurred to him that this might be one of the best days of his life because he suddenly saw possibilities where he had never seen them before.

Chapter Ten

Chandler was awake before dawn on the barn-raising day, which was not typical. There was no herd of cows to milk like when his father was alive, and he didn't have to be on a jobsite by seven. He didn't have a job anymore, which was daunting and exhilarating at the same time. Four days ago, he'd called his boss in Illinois and told him he wouldn't be returning. He thanked him for a good job with fair wages but explained that he needed to remain in Delaware to care for his aging mother. Which was true. He *did* want to be here for her.

The person Chandler did not mention during the phone call was Henrietta Koffman. His Henry…at least the woman he prayed would be his Henry someday. What would he have said to his old boss? That he met a woman he could see himself marrying, but they weren't dating? And then there was the matter of being required to be baptized into the church to marry her. He wasn't even sure she wanted to marry him. It was likely foolish to have quit his job with so many unknowns, but it had felt right, so he'd done it. Now he greeted each morning with a mixture of excitement and apprehension. He'd never felt so unmoored, not even when he'd left Delaware in the middle of the night. But at the same time, he felt a comfort in that invisible thread that kept him here. The thread was connected to Henry but also to his mother, his community, his church and God.

By the time his mother had come downstairs that Saturday morning, Chandler had already dressed, fed the livestock and made coffee for them. The night before, they had discussed whether she would go with him early or travel with the neighbors midmorning. By the time he poured coffee for her, she had decided to come midmorning, so Chandler took the horse and buggy and traveled to the Hershberger farm in Honeycomb. He had wanted to pick Henry up on his way, but she'd refused his invitation. She insisted that she would not be seen alone in a buggy with him until she severed any romantic ties, real or imagined, with Sam.

The week between his first church service in eight years and the barn raising had gone well between Henry and him. They'd worked long hours each day. They'd replaced the decades-old plumbing, painted the walls a buttercup yellow, repaired and repainted the shelving in the walk-in pantry. Other than the installation of the cabinets, there was little else to do but a few finishing touches, then his mother would have the brand-new kitchen she had always dreamed of. And if things went well in the coming days, Chandler might have a girlfriend.

He and Henry had talked for hours each day, and while she said she wouldn't discuss officially walking out together until she talked with Sam, their conversations had circled that premise. Henry had told him flat out that she would not leave her church, not for any man, and without hesitation, he had countered with his intention to be baptized. He had no idea what had made him say such a thing.

Sunday, as he and his *mam* had prepared to leave the Mast farm, Bishop Cyrus had joined them in the barnyard and asked if he would be willing to visit him later in the week to talk. Chandler had gone to see him Wednesday after work, and their conversation had been affable enough that he'd agreed to meet with the spiritual leader again. However, he had not committed to anything. He only agreed to listen to what the man had to say to explore the possibility. His mother had told him how proud she was of him and gushed about how his return had answered her prayers to the point that he hadn't had the heart to remind her that he had not committed to staying yet. He and the bishop were only talking. He didn't mention to her that he and Henry were also talking about their future in a roundabout way, but he had a feeling his mother already suspected that.

Chandler was one of the first men to arrive at the Hershberger farm, and even though they'd never met, the family greeted him as if they were old friends. He wasn't even sure they knew he had left the church. Certainly, his physical appearance didn't suggest it. He wore his old Amish work clothes and a wide-brimmed straw hat to keep the sun off his face and neck. Saul Hershberger introduced Chandler to three other men, and while they talked, waiting for others, his wife, Dotty, served coffee and homemade strawberry strudel. Saul explained the basics of the plan for the day and showed him a list of the expected volunteers and their assignments. While eating a second piece of strudel at Dotty's insistence, Chandler perused the list and was pleased to see that he, Sam and Henry had all been assigned to build the walls in an open field a short distance from the barn. The walls would later be nailed into place.

As the sun rose higher in the sky and the

morning air grew warmer and more humid, horse-drawn buggies and wagons began to roll up the long lane. Within half an hour, the wide front porch of the farmhouse, which was serving as a volunteer staging area, was alive with the sound of male laughter and camaraderie. After coffee was drunk and strudel consumed, the men began to head for the new barn site to get started on their assigned tasks. With no sign of Henry yet, Chandler began to worry.

Had she changed her mind about attending the barn raising? Had she changed her mind about *him*? Or maybe he had misinterpreted what she told him. He thought she had implied she'd be open to dating him with the intention of marriage once she had broken things off with Sam. However, he assumed neither had come out and said it out of respect for Sam. Had it been wishful thinking when he understood her words and actions to mean she was interested in him in a romantic way? He was being irrational, but when he finally saw Henry walking across the grass toward him, he heaved a sigh of relief. She wore a blue dress, work boots and a scarf over her hair, tied at her nape, and carried a well-used wooden toolbox.

"I was afraid you weren't coming," Chandler said when she approached.

She pulled a face. "Why wouldn't I come? I

was running late because *Dat* wanted to ride with me, but then he couldn't find his boots, and Eleanor insisted he couldn't wear his slippers. Of course, I was coming. Do you not know me any better than that? I wouldn't miss a barn raising." She smiled at him and lowered her voice as she set the toolbox down. "Or spending time with you."

Her blue-eyed gaze held his, and all his concerns evaporated like the morning dew from the grass. He had *not* imagined their attraction; he heard it in her voice and saw it in her eyes.

"Henry, good to see you." Saul Hershberger walked over to them. "I hear Chandler's been working with you on his mother's house. You mind teaming up with him and building some partition walls?"

She smiled at the older man, whose long, dark beard was beginning to show traces of gray. "*Nay*, not at all."

Saul handed her a sheet of paper. "Interior tack room walls. The specs are all there. I'm glad you're willing to help, Henry." He glanced toward a gaggle of white *kapps* entering the kitchen by a side door. "I wouldn't hold it against you if you'd decided to join the women, though."

"*Nay*, I want to be a part of the build. But I can only work in the morning. I promised Eleanor that I'd help clean up the midday meal and keep an eye on our *dat*."

"There you are."

Chandler looked up to see Sam striding toward them, a tool belt slung over his shoulder. "I looked for you in the kitchen," he told Henry.

She gave him a tight smile. "And yet I'm here." She opened her arms wide.

"Sam, glad you made it," Saul said, pulling through his papers. "I've got you and your brothers John and Mark assigned to building the exterior west wall." He handed Sam a sheet of paper.

"Saul! We got a question here," a man Chandler didn't know called.

"Let me know if you have any questions, Sam," Saul instructed and walked away.

Sam looked at Chandler, then Henry. "You're doing this?" he asked. "Working on the barn instead of being in the kitchen with the women?"

"*Ya*, for the morning, at least." She glanced down and then back at Sam. "I hope you had a good week on the job at the beach."

He nodded, then glanced around. "Here come my brothers. Guess we best get to work."

Chandler stood beside Henry and watched Sam go. "You think he knows you want to break things off?" he asked her quietly.

"How could he not?"

Chandler wanted to ask her when she intended to talk to him. He was eager to know when she would set herself free from Sam, but he didn't want her to think he was pushing her. She needed to do it in her own time, and he knew she didn't want anyone telling her what to do. Not on this matter or any other.

Henry sighed, plucked the paper from his hand and walked off the porch. "You coming?" she called over her shoulder.

He watched her go, thinking how blessed he was to be there today helping folks and working beside Henry. In his meeting with the bishop, the older man suggested that he ease back into the structure of his faith by observing the evidence of God's presence around him. The advice had seemed odd at the time, but standing there on the porch steps, he felt, heard and saw God all around him. The ripple of the fabric of Henry's dress, the smell of freshly cut grass and the laughter of the women floating through the kitchen windows were all sweet signs of His presence, and Chandler found himself eager to see what the day would bring.

Henry had never built a partition wall, only replaced rotted portions of one, but thankfully, Chandler had. Even though he took the lead on building the three non-weight-bearing walls that would attach to an outer wall of the barn, he made it feel as if she was a part of the process every step of the way. His instructions were simple, clear and never condescending, and he seemed to enjoy teaching her a new skill.

After verifying the measurements Saul Hershberger had provided, Chandler outlined the steps to building a partition wall, and they went to work cutting the necessary pieces. Several generators and power tools had been brought in to speed up the process and were set up in a central location. Henry had only used power tools a couple of times because she didn't own any, so she found it thrilling to cut the two-by-fours to the correct lengths with them.

As she and Chandler worked, they talked about everything, as they had in his mother's kitchen every workday. Sometimes the subject was silly, like what kinds of antics they got into trouble for when they were children, but often it was more serious. She sensed they were feeling each other out, trying to ensure their attraction wasn't superficial. They talked about how annual warmer temperatures affected crops and whether bishops were being forced to become more lenient to retain their flocks. They discussed the plague of drugs, alcohol and tobacco in Amish communities, and Chandler offered his insight.

"So you saw it out west, too? Did you work

with a lot of Amish?" Henry asked as she marked two-by-fours for cutting into the smaller pieces that would make the header for the door to a tack room.

"It depended on the job," Chandler told her as he laid out the wood they'd already cut so they could assemble the wall.

The plan was to build all three walls and attach them to one of the barn's exterior walls after they broke for the midday meal. Henry tried not to be disappointed that she wouldn't be present for the raising of the walls she helped build, but she wasn't resentful. Not about taking her turn with her father, at least. The kitchen cleanup she could do without.

"Some jobs, more than half the crew were Amish." He stood up and removed his straw hat to wipe the perspiration from his forehead with a handkerchief. "Other jobs, there were none. It depended on the location and how close we were to Amish settlements."

"Do you think working with *Englishers* makes Amish men want to try the beer and cigarettes?" she asked. She was so unfamiliar with recreational drugs that she didn't know how to ask about them.

"Maybe some men," he said thoughtfully. "Some are more curious than others, and there was certainly more opportunity for the Amish men if they were working on an English crew. I worked with this one guy, Travis. Englisher. I'd ride with him into town to pick up lunch sometimes, and he'd always buy beer so he'd have it the minute it was quitting time."

Henry stood up to ease the tightness in her back and took a drink from a water bottle that one of Jon Yoder's girls had brought by a few minutes ago. It was a beautiful cloudless day, but the temperature was already in the high seventies. "You said you drank alcohol. Too much. Is that why you did it? Because the *Englishers* did?"

He turned to look at her. His handsome face was thoughtful, and she imagined what it would be like to sit across the breakfast table from him every morning for the rest of her life. The idea was exciting but scary, too. She wanted a husband and a family, but she wanted to marry a man who accepted her for who she was. Was it too much to hope and pray for Chandler to be that man?

"I tried beer out of curiosity," Chandler admitted. "You know, you leave home, you want to do all the things you weren't permitted." He frowned. "It didn't even taste good at first. But…after a while I liked the way it made me feel. It made it easier to forget things."

"Like what?" she asked.

He shrugged. "Being homesick. Wondering

if I made the right decision leaving." His voice grew husky with emotion. "Worrying about my mother, my family."

She nodded and walked over to him, sipping from the water bottle. "Then why'd you quit?"

"Because eventually, I started to feel worse instead of better. Beer wasn't helping me forget—it was only postponing the emotions I needed to deal with. And I saw what it did to people I knew. Guys I worked with. At least three over the years got fired for drinking. First, they'd come to work hungover or late, and eventually, they'd start missing work altogether. Then they didn't have a job."

"What does *hungover* mean?" she asked as she spotted Sam across the yard watching her. Watching them. She returned her attention to Chandler.

"It's this sick feeling you have the next day. Your head hurts, and sometimes your whole body. You're thirsty but sick to your stomach, so you're afraid to drink much water."

She frowned. "Sounds awful."

He nodded. "It is."

She met his gaze, and he grinned at her. "What?" she asked, unable to resist smiling back.

"I didn't say anything." His tone was teasing.

"But you're looking at me. And you've got a big smile on your face."

"What? I can't smile at you?"

She looked at him suspiciously. "Have I got dirt on my face or something?" She rubbed her cheek with the back of her hand.

"No, but if you did, it wouldn't matter. I like talking to you. And even with dirt on your face, you'd still be the prettiest woman here."

She felt herself blush. "You'd best not say things like that. Sam's keeping an eye on us." He started to turn in Sam's direction, but she said, *"Don't."*

He froze.

"I think Sam suspects something, and I don't want to make this harder for him than it's already going to be," she told him. "I don't want to hurt him."

"I know you don't. And neither do I."

"Oh no," she breathed. "Here he comes."

"Does he look upset?" Chandler asked.

She groaned. "I don't know. But he's coming straight for us."

Chandler picked up his hammer and squatted to sink a nail. Henry checked her measurement before carrying a two-by-four to the electric miter saw.

"How's it going?" Sam asked when he reached them. He chewed on a piece of beef jerky in his hand.

"Goot," Chandler answered without looking up as he hammered another nail into place.

Sam nodded slowly, then turned to Henry. "Can we talk?"

His words so surprised her that she stared at him for a moment. He had never asked her to talk before. "Um... *Ya*, of course."

"Mind if I borrow your building partner here?" Sam asked Chandler.

Chandler avoided Henry's gaze, which was good because if he looked at her, she would feel guiltier than she already did. Not that she and Chandler had done anything wrong or inappropriate. They hadn't directly discussed walking out together, but she still felt uncomfortable.

"Fine by me," Chandler said, lowering his head to concentrate on what he was doing.

Sam walked away, and Henry hurried to catch up. They strolled through freshly cut grass toward a pond beyond the location of the new barn.

"I saw you two," Sam said when they were out of earshot of his buddy. He pulled a bag of beef jerky from his pocket and fished a piece.

"What?" Henry asked, knowing full well they hadn't done anything unfitting. "Saw us what? We've been building the walls."

"Talking," Sam said, continuing to walk. He didn't look at her. "I saw you laughing. Smiling at each other." He kicked a tuft of grass. "You like him, and he likes you." His tone was tense but not angry.

"We haven't done anything wrong," she told him.

He stopped. Chewed more of his jerky. "I know you wouldn't, and Chandler wouldn't, either. Because you're not like that. But…it doesn't matter. It's still there, plain to see."

"What's there?" she asked, pulling at the neckline of her blue dress. It was only seventy-eight degrees outside, but it felt hotter than that.

"He likes you. And you like him."

Henry's first impulse was to disagree, but instead, she simply said, "I'm sorry, Sam." And she was. She was sorry to hurt him this way. She was sorry he wasn't the one who stirred these feelings inside her because that would be easier. Sam was already a church member, a man approved of by her family. Sam was the man her sisters wanted her to marry. But Sam wasn't Chandler, and while she didn't understand her feelings for him, she knew she didn't feel the same about Sam. She knew she never would.

Sam cleared his throat. "I guess what I'm trying to say is that I'm breaking up with you."

His words caught her completely off guard, and it took her a moment to respond. "You can't break up with me," she said, trying to add levity to the conversation. "I never agreed to walk out with you."

They both chuckled, and a lump of emotion rose in her throat. She glanced away, fearing she might tear up. Why was she sad? She should be happy. She *was* happy, but sad too because she didn't like disappointing Sam or her family.

"Okay. I release you," he said firmly. "From whatever we had or didn't have."

She moved in front of him and watched him chew on another piece of beef jerky. His Adam's apple bobbed as he swallowed.

"You're being so nice about this," she said. "I almost wish you weren't. I almost wish you would be angry, maybe shout at me."

"Not my way."

She smiled sadly. "No, it isn't, is it? Which is one of the many reasons you're going to find the right woman for you. A woman meant to be your wife."

"Guess we'll see about that. But I want to tell you if things don't work out between you... If Chandler doesn't stay or you decide he's not the one for you, I'll still marry you, Henrietta."

"Sam, I wouldn't expect you to marry me. Not after I—" She didn't go any further because she didn't know how to describe what she'd done. Had she fallen in love with his best friend?

"I'm serious," he told her, taking another bite. "Things don't work out with my buddy, you come back to me, and I'll have you for my wife."

She wanted to argue with him that that was ridiculous. Even if things didn't work out between her and Chandler, taking her back would be a mistake. He'd be a fool to marry her always knowing he was her second choice. But instead, she thanked him for his kindness. She watched him walk away in the direction of the house, then headed toward Chandler, her heart feeling much lighter than it had a few minutes ago.

When she approached, he rose from where he was kneeling, cutting a plank. "You break with him?"

"Nay." She tried hard not to smile even though she was excited inside. Now she was free to explore her feelings with Chandler and see where they went. If he continued on the path of baptism, of course. That was non-negotiable.

"You didn't?" Chandler's face fell.

"Nay." She sighed, starting to feel guilty teasing him this way. He looked like a boy who'd just lost his puppy. "I didn't break up with him…because he broke up with me!"

Chandler's eyes lit up, and he broke into a grin. "Really?"

She nodded. "He said it was clear I didn't

have feelings for him, and…" She hesitated, not sure she was ready to say this. But why wouldn't she be? There was no denying her and Chandler's attraction to each other; she was no longer a schoolgirl. She had to recognize her feelings and be willing to share them with a man who felt the same way.

"And?" he asked. "And what?"

"And I'm free to walk out with someone else." She cut her eyes at him. "If someone were to ask me. Or if I was to ask him," she added saucily.

His blue eyes were eager. "Know anyone you'd like to ask?"

She shrugged. "Can I think about it?"

"Certainly not. I need to move quickly before someone else scoops you up. So would you?" He took a step closer to her. "Walk out with me? Be my girl?"

She reached out and clasped his hand, not caring who might see them. "*Ya*, I'd like to be your girl, but only if you'll be my beau." Suddenly she felt shy.

"So it's decided," he whispered. He met her gaze, and she wasn't certain which of them was more pleased.

Chapter Eleven

Henry stood in the center of Edee's kitchen listening to the sweet sound of organized chaos as women bustled about tidying, talking and laughing. It was the first visiting Sunday gathering Edee had hosted in a year. The widow was enjoying the fuss everyone was making over the renovation almost as much as she relished seeing folks officially welcome her son into the Amish community of Kent County.

Three barefoot girls, barely out of diapers, in pink tab dresses and white *kapps* circled the table heavily laden with food. When their mother chastised them for causing a commotion in their neighbor's home, they darted down the hallway giggling. Watching the little ones created a strange ache in Henry's chest, and she wondered if it was caused by her childhood memories of being with her sisters. Or the hope of having her own daughters someday.

"You'll go home if you can't behave," Dory

Swartzentruber warned her twins and their older sister as they disappeared into another room, chasing one of the barn cats that had accidentally been let inside in the day's commotion.

Edee originally had intended to visit outside under the shade of the live oaks in her backyard, but when a thundershower rolled in, everyone had scooped up the nearest plate or bowl of food or stray child and run for the house. The men and boys had taken shelter on the large porch, leaving the women to deal with the food and youngest children and to spend time together without their men underfoot.

At the sink, Millie washed dishes, giggling with their friend Annie, who was drying them. From the bright red of her sister's round cheeks, Henry suspected they were talking about Millie and Elden's news. In the fall, the newlyweds would be expecting their first child, and the Koffman family was beyond excited. However, they had agreed not to tell their father yet because, for one thing, he would tell everyone he met, which was inappropriate since pregnancies weren't discussed publicly. And for another, once he knew he was expecting his first grandchild, he'd ask when the baby was arriving every day for the next five months.

Henry's gaze moved from Millie, past Jane

and Beth, who were busy making to-go bags for the dozens of homemade cookies they'd brought, and settled on Eleanor. Their oldest sister stood near the pantry door, arms crossed, as she spoke softly with Edee. There were tears in Eleanor's eyes, and Henry felt guilty for being happy when her sister was so sad.

Her best friend, Sara, had passed away a week ago, leaving her husband and two children behind. Sara's diabetes had led to kidney failure, and the Lord had taken her home to heaven. Sara had been sick in bed for weeks, unable to care for her family. *Gott* truly did know best, but that didn't make it any easier for those left behind. Ellie had been a rock to the family since her beloved friend's passing, spending as much time with Sara's family as her own. Today, however, the stress of trying to run two households showed on her face, and Henry's heart ached for her sister. For all those who had loved Sara.

Suddenly, the humid kitchen felt overly warm, and Henry moved to the bay of windows. She slid one up, pleased with how smoothly it glided open. The sounds of men and boys drifted in with the scent of the first summer rain shower and wet grass.

"*Danki*, Henry," Edee called from the far side of the room. "I was just about to do that." The widow smiled proudly. "They open and close so easily, I find myself doing it just for the fun of it!"

Henry smiled as she nodded in response, and Edee returned to her quiet conversation with Eleanor. After moving to the far end of the row of windows, Henry unlatched another.

As she pushed it upward, she heard a male voice from very near. "About time you came to the window." It was Chandler. "I've been trying to get your attention for ten minutes," he continued, his words soft enough that no one else could hear him. "Save me. I'm tired of listening to the same conversations we were having eight years ago when I left."

She smiled, leaning one way and then the other. She couldn't see him. She glanced over her shoulder to see if any women were watching her, but no one seemed to be. "Which conversation? The one about the poor harvest to be expected this fall or the rise in fertilizer prices?"

"Both." He stepped in front of the window and pressed his nose to the screen. "Want to go for a walk? I want to hold your hand," he added in a whisper.

She couldn't stop smiling. Her entire life had changed in the last month. She and Chandler had finished the renovation, and she now officially had a beau. Chandler had been seeing her uncle at least twice a week for guidance and counseling, and she was hoping he would soon choose a date for his baptism. Once he was baptized, they'd be free to marry when they were ready. They had seen each other every day but one since the barn raising, and when they weren't together, Henry felt as if she were missing a part of herself. She still couldn't believe she had fallen in love or someone had fallen in love with her. They'd not said the words to each other yet, but she felt them in her heart and saw them in his blue eyes each time she gazed into them. And in his eyes, she felt he accepted her for who she was, even if she would never fit into the mold of what some believed to be a proper Old Order wife and mother.

"Come on, you know you want to," Chandler cajoled from outside the window.

"But it's raining," she argued, though only half-heartedly.

"It's not. It stopped fifteen minutes ago, and the sun is trying to peek out from the clouds. I wouldn't be surprised if we saw a rainbow."

"I don't know," she hedged. "There are dishes still to be washed, and I should check on *Dat*."

He peered in the window. "Looks to me like Millie and Annie have the dishes under control, and Felty walked to the barn with Bishop Cyrus to look at our new kittens."

She nibbled on her bottom lip in indecision. She wanted to go with him, but what would her aunt say about her "gallivanting about with a man, unchaperoned"? That was what she'd said the previous week when she bumped into Chandler and her shopping in Dover. The fact that Edee was one aisle over hadn't seemed to matter.

"Come on. We haven't had a minute to ourselves today," Chandler pressed. "I miss you, Henry. If you don't come outside right now, I'll start calling you *Henny*," he teased playfully.

She laughed. "You most certainly will not." She looked at the men still gathered on the porch and spotted her two brothers-in-law and several men from Rose Valley, all husbands and sons-in-law of Edee's friends. "Someone will see us," she whispered. Chandler was so close, with only the screen between them, that she could smell his shaving soap and feel the warmth of his skin.

"Go out the front door. No one will be the wiser." He tapped on the windowsill. "I'll meet you at the hydrangea bushes." Then he was gone.

Henry nonchalantly walked through the kitchen, her heart aflutter, looking to see which of her sisters noticed her. But no one paid her any mind, and she slipped out the front door without a soul noticing her. She was halfway across the side yard when she spotted Chandler patiently waiting for her at the designated meeting place. When she reached him, he put out his hand, and she accepted it. They walked side by side in comfortable silence until they were beyond the house and barnyard.

"Where are we going?" she asked.

"I thought we'd walk down to the pond." He pointed across an open meadow that led to a copse of trees that hid the body of water. "I repaired the old rowboat Joe and I used to fish in. We could try it out, see if it springs another leak."

"And let my aunt see me soaked to the bone, walking back across the field with my beau? *Danki, nay.* I'll not put that stress on Ellie right now. Judy sat for two hours in our kitchen the other day, telling her how improper it was for us to buy curtain rods together."

He laughed. "For my mother? And she was with us!"

Henry shook her head slowly, enjoying the feel of his hand in hers. She'd never held hands with a man before. It never occurred to her that it could feel so good. So right. "I'm simply telling you what she told Eleanor. For *two hours.*"

"Aw, she's not so bad. She invited me to supper next week and said I should bring you and my *mam*."

"Oh, dear." Henry looked up. They were nearing the trees, and the path had grown narrower, forcing them to walk closer together. "I won't be able to make it. I'm busy. So busy."

He made a face at her. "I didn't even tell you what night it was yet."

"Doesn't matter. I don't like rabbit."

He looked at her quizzically. "Rabbit?"

"*Hasenpfeffer*. It's her specialty. And her rabbits are domestic, not wild. She raises them, and then she eats them. Big, fat, white bunnies. The whole house is covered in fluffy white doilies. She tans the hides herself. She gifted a box of them to my sisters when they wed. I imagine there's a bundle waiting for me as well." She cut her eyes at him. "Should you make good on your talk of marrying me someday, your house will also be covered in bunny doilies."

He was laughing so hard now that tears filled his eyes. "I cannot abide *hasenpfeffer*, but now I can't wait to see the doilies." He wiped at his eyes with a handkerchief he pulled from his pants pocket. "As for making good on my talk of wedding you, it's not just talking." He stopped, suddenly growing serious, and drew her hand to his chest. "I want to marry you,

Henry. I want to marry you because I love you and—"

The sound of voices startled them both, and they turned to see her sister Cora and her beau, Tobit, walking out of the cover of the trees. "Cora?" Henry pulled her hand from Chandler's. "Tobit. I... I didn't realize you had walked to the pond."

Her sister's face turned bright red, and she dropped her beau's hand. Physical displays of affection were meant for the privacy of marriage. Some couples were affectionate before marriage, but it wasn't discussed and certainly wasn't seen.

Cora and Henry met each other's gazes, and both smiled with embarrassment. *Caught*, Henry thought as her cheeks grew warm. Of course, it would have been foolish for anyone to think Tobit and Cora weren't holding hands privately. Tobit, a local schoolteacher, had recently asked Cora for her hand in marriage, and they were planning to wed in August before the new term began.

Her sister looked up at Tobit, a big bear of a man to Cora's petite frame, and the two smiled at each other. Henry had witnessed their smiles before, but now that she had fallen in love, she understood the subtle exchanges between couples.

"We were, um, taking a walk," Cora said.

"*Ya*, us, too," Henry replied before pressing her lips together to keep from smiling again.

"Good time for a walk. Between rain showers," Chandler offered, sliding his hands casually into his pants pockets.

Tobit nodded. "True enough," he added awkwardly.

"Well." Cora put her hands together. "Enjoy your walk." She passed Henry and Chandler, and Tobit followed her.

Henry and Chandler fell into step, side by side, and didn't speak until they walked into the cluster of trees surrounding the pond and out of view of her sister.

"Well, that was awkward," Henry breathed.

Chandler took her hand in his again. "Why's that?"

She looked at him, unable to believe what he'd just said. "Because they saw us holding hands, and we saw them doing the same."

He shrugged. "It's innocent enough, don't you think?" He brushed her hand rhythmically with his thumb. "And nothing like what you see in the *English* world. I think I'm still scarred by the inappropriate sights I've seen."

Henry didn't know what got into her, but she laughed. "I'm sorry. I shouldn't." She covered her mouth with her hand. "How terrible for you."

He shrugged. "In some ways, *ya*. But, you know something? I've spent a lot of time thinking over the last few weeks, and having lived out there in the *English* world—" he glanced at her "—it's made me appreciate our life here. Appreciate our rules. Now, instead of seeing them as holding us back, I see them as... I don't know. Protecting us, maybe?" He hesitated, still holding her gaze. "Does that make sense?"

"It does. Is that something my uncle told you?"

"*Nay*. Our time together isn't like that. He asks me questions and then listens. Really listens to me. Never once since I started talking with him has he told me I had to return to the church. He hasn't told me I *had* to do anything. He reminds me that *Gott* gives us free will. Bishop Cyrus is good at what he does. He understands that this is my journey and I have to find my way back on my own."

They halted where the wide path split, one footpath going in the direction of a large weeping willow tree. The other led toward the quarter-acre pond, where a wooden rowboat rested on the grassy bank. "I'm glad you're finding your way back, Chandler."

"I am, too," he told her. He stopped and turned to face her, taking her other hand so he could hold both. "Because as I was about to say before your sister and her fiancé appeared..."

He took a deep breath and looked into her eyes. "I'm glad I'm finding my way back because I love you, Henry. I'd do anything to spend the rest of my life with you."

"You have to do this for yourself, Chandler. Not for me."

"I *am* doing it for me. I wasn't happy out there, Henry. Not like I thought I would be. Now that I'm back, I want to be a better man for myself and you. I hope to be the man you'll want to marry very soon. I hope I'll reach the point where Bishop Cyrus will be willing to baptize me."

Henry felt her eyes grow scratchy with emotion, and she swallowed hard. She wasn't good at talking like this. About her feelings. And it wasn't as if she'd had any practice doing it, but she wanted to tell him how proud she was of him for committing to finding his way home to his faith. She wanted to tell him she loved him, too.

Slowly, she gazed into his eyes. She was going to tell him she loved him, too, but suddenly she was afraid to say it. She knew she loved him, but saying it would make her more vulnerable, and that was frightening. Instead, she said, "Of course, my uncle will baptize you. That's what bishops do."

"But..." He closed his eyes for a moment, hesitated, then opened them. "But what if the things I've done, the things I've seen... Henry, what if I'm not good enough to be accepted into the church?"

He looked scared now, which scared her. It had never occurred to her that he might have doubts at this point. Not weeks after he began meeting with their bishop. She never considered that her plan for him to be baptized and for them to marry wouldn't work out, and she didn't know what to do with that. She didn't know how to acknowledge his fears or comfort him. Instead, she pulled her hands from his and said, "Now you're being silly."

"No, no, I'm not, Henry. I'm being realistic."

"Are you saying you're not sure about staying? About wanting to marry me?"

"That's not what I'm saying at all. What I'm trying to tell you, and saying it poorly is that—"

"Chandler!" someone shouted from the meadow beyond the trees. "Chandler!" It was Tobit's booming voice. He burst through the trees at a run. "You have to come quick!"

"What is it?" Chandler called, alarm in his voice. "What's wrong?"

"Your *mudder*," Tobit hollered, breathing heavily from running. "She's fallen and hurt herself. She needs to go to the hospital."

Chandler looked at Henry, his eyes wild with fear.

She laid her hand on his arm. "Go," she told

him. "Run. I'll be there quick as I can." She gave him a gentle push, and he took off.

Chandler paced his mother's hospital room as Henry lifted a can of pop to help Edee drink it. His *mam* sat up in bed in a patient gown with a sheet around her shoulders for modesty. While waiting for the ambulance, someone had the forethought to grab a scarf for her to replace her prayer *kapp*, knowing she would have to lie down for the ride into Dover. Switching out her head coverings, Henry had explained to him as he drove behind the ambulance in his truck, prevented her *kapp* from getting squished. Even worse, she said, medical personnel might try to remove it, not understanding how sacred it was to a woman.

Chandler was so thankful Henry had come with them to the hospital. Otherwise, he wasn't sure how well he would have navigated the last few hours. It was odd how he had lived in the *English* world for eight years, yet it was Henry who knew what to do and say in this situation. When she had seen he was struggling, she'd taken over completely, talking with the doctors and his mother, translating when necessary so he didn't have to.

Chandler didn't know what was wrong with him. He didn't understand why he was such an emotional wreck. His *mam* was going to be okay. Her upper arm bone had a clean break and had already been set and plastered. Henry and the nursing staff had assured him several times that the slight irregularity in her heartbeat was likely nothing to be too concerned about and could be dealt with by a follow-up appointment with her cardiologist. Henry said they were only keeping his mother overnight to be cautious and that if nothing unexpected occurred, she'd be released first thing the next morning. All good news. But then he looked at his mother in the hospital bed and was overcome with anxiety again.

She was hooked up to a heart monitor with an IV in her arm, just in case. He had asked the nurse, "In case of what?" but both *his mam* and Henry had shushed him, and he hadn't gotten an answer.

Chandler groaned and paced faster. Seeing his *mam* in the bed, the area around her right eye turning blacker by the moment, made him want to cry. Hearing the steady beat of her heart on the monitor made his own beat loudly in his ears. While trying his best to look and sound calm, he'd already had to step out into the hall to catch his breath, and he feared he might have to do so again.

He watched Henry adjust the pillow under

his mother's arm, which was in a cast from her wrist to her shoulder. She was so good with her, gentle and tender but never smothering. This was a different side of Henry than the one he'd gotten to know since he arrived two months ago. He loved her for who she was, as she was, but this quintessentially feminine side—or what others saw as feminine—was new. And it made him love her even more for being so complex. Each day since the barn raising when they'd committed to each other, he learned something new about her. It was like peeling the layers of an onion. Each time he thought he knew her, he found a more intricate portion of her personality beneath.

Watching her right now, surrounded by such a confusing, intimidating *English* world, he saw Henry fitting in as well as anyone. Better than him, certainly. That made him feel unworthy. Was she too good for him, too perfect? Would she ever be content with a simple man like him? She was smarter and more capable than he was. If they married, would she soon feel trapped? She seemed happy now, but how long would that last? And while he intended to be baptized, what if he faltered? What if he couldn't be the man she wanted him to be? Maybe he didn't deserve a woman like Henry. He had left the church, run away and abandoned his family. What Amish man did such a thing?

A sweat broke out on his forehead, and he walked to the window to look out over the hospital's roof and a parking lot in the distance. He watched raindrops hit the glass. There were better Amish out there than him. Sam certainly was. Was he wrong about the two of them? Had he told her and Sam that they weren't well matched for his gain? Had he said those things because he loved and wanted her for himself?

A knock on the room's open door startled Chandler, who turned around. It was Henry's sister Eleanor. She smiled at him, her face a mask of kindness, and all he could think was, *do I truly deserve this family?*

"Ellie." Henry popped up from the bedside chair. "Come in."

"*Ya*, come in," his mother echoed.

"I won't stay but a moment. I brought these for you from our garden." She walked in carrying a large bunch of flowers wrapped in a newspaper. "And a jar, too," she said, indicating the bag on her shoulder. "And I have the things you asked for from your house. And a few others I thought you might want. Toiletries and such."

"Oh, goodness, that wasn't necessary," his

mother said. But she was beaming and pleased by the attention.

"Let me take the bag." Henry slipped it off her sister's shoulder. "I'll put the things in her bedside drawer. Here you go." She handed the blue quart jar to Eleanor.

"I'll add water." Eleanor smiled at his mother. "Where would you like them, Edee? Beside the bed or here?" She indicated a shelf on the wall beneath the TV at the foot of the bed.

"Oh, yes, there. How beautiful. Cosmos, snapdragons, yarrow," his *mam* observed.

"We planted half an acre of flowers for cutting this spring," Eleanor explained as she arranged the flowers in the jar and then carried it to the sink to add water. "They sell very well in the store," she explained over her shoulder. "We love sharing them with as many folks as we can."

"You still shouldn't have," his mother chastised kindly. "Please tell me you didn't drive your buggy all the way here from Honeycomb to bring me my brush and flowers."

"*Nay*, I did not." Eleanor set the colorful bouquet on the shelf. "A driver brought me. I thought we could give Henry a ride home so Chandler would be free to stay here as long as he liked." She glanced at him.

He nodded but said nothing, not fully trusting his voice. He wasn't sure he should be depended upon to know if his mother needed him. Or *what* she needed, he thought, a panicky feeling in his chest. Maybe it was Henry who ought to stay and not him. Maybe it would be best if he got in his truck, drove away and kept driving until he crossed the state line and Delaware was behind him. Maybe that would be best for everyone.

Having tucked the items from Eleanor's bag into the drawers of the nightstand, Henry said, "I think that's wise that I go home with Ellie."

"I certainly don't need Chandler to stay," his mother huffed. "I don't need anyone to stay. I'm fine." She smoothed the white cotton blanket over her with her good hand. "All this fuss. You heard the doctor, Henry. I can go home first thing tomorrow. You should all go and leave me to get some rest."

Henry looked to Chandler. "I'll go with Ellie if that's okay. She's all settled in for the night." She glanced at his *mam*, then back at him.

Henry's smile was so sweet that it broke his heart to think he might break hers if he couldn't be the man she wanted him to be. "Of course. Fine," he mumbled.

Eleanor had walked to the bedside and covered his *mam*'s hand with hers. "We'll all include you in our prayers tonight, Edee. I'll call on you in a couple of days to see how you're making out."

"I'm going to be just fine," his mother harrumphed. "But, *danki*. For everything. You're a fine family, you Koffmans, and we're blessed to have you in our lives, aren't we, *sohn*?" She looked at him.

"Blessed," he repeated.

"*Goot*, well—" Eleanor walked to the door. "I'll wait for you out by the elevator, Henry. I told the driver we wouldn't be long."

Eleanor said good-night, and when Henry stopped at the door and looked at him expectantly, he moved toward her, feeling as if his feet were weighted down with cement.

When he got closer, Henry said softly, "You *oll recht*?" Her blue-eyed gaze searched his.

He nodded. "Fine." He studied his boots. "The nurse said I should come first thing in the morning. To pick her up. Could you be here? I'm not good with this sort of thing. Seven o'clock, okay?"

"Of course," she told him, concern in her voice. "I'll wait for you at the store." Then she spoke more quietly. "You sure you're okay?"

He nodded, still not looking at her.

"She's going to be fine," Henry whispered. "Don't worry. Go home and get some sleep."

He nodded.

"Good night, Edee," Henry called. "I'll see you in the morning."

"*Danki*, dear. For all you've done," she answered cheerfully.

Henry met Chandler's gaze. "See you in the morning," she whispered.

She walked out of the hospital room into the brightly lit hallway, and he wondered if he had made a terrible mistake ever coming home.

Chapter Twelve

At seven the next morning, Henry stood on the front porch of their store waiting for Chandler to pick her up so they could fetch his mother from the hospital. She didn't become overly concerned until seven fifteen, when he still wasn't there. At seven-twenty, she went into the store and used the phone to call his cell. There was no answer.

Where was he? Had he overslept? She assumed he was coming for her in his truck. What if he'd been in a car accident?

It was possible, but it didn't seem likely as there was little traffic that time of day between Rose Valley and Honeycomb. She offered a quick prayer for his safety and pushed that possibility from her mind. There had to be another explanation.

She debated calling Edee to be sure she hadn't mixed up the plans. Maybe Chandler was coming for her *after* he picked up his mother? But something in the pit of her stomach warned her not to make that call. There was no need to worry Edee unnecessarily; surely he was running late for some mundane reason. But she tried his cell three more times: the first two, she left a message. The third time she attempted to contact him, a voice told her that his mailbox was full. She considered her next move for only a moment. Deciding she should find her way to the hospital, she looked at a list taped to the wall and again picked up the phone. She tried two drivers: one didn't answer, and the other couldn't take her until the afternoon. She considered hitching up a buggy and going into town herself, but if there was a mix-up and Chandler was already at the hospital, that would only complicate things. The buggy would take longer than a motor vehicle, and right now she felt like she had to get to the hospital quickly. Edee had been annoyed that she had to stay the night, so Henry knew she'd be eager to be discharged.

After wracking her brain for another moment, Henry made another phone call. Her sister Beth's Mennonite friend Rosie was delighted to be asked to drive somewhere. Rosie had only recently gotten her license and was eager to use it. Forty-five minutes later, Henry walked into Edee's hospital room.

The widow was seated in a chair beside the bed and alone. She was fully dressed and ready to go. "You're late," she remarked when Henry walked in.

"I'm sorry."

"You would think a person wouldn't be late with a motorcar." Edee rose from the chair, waving Henry away with her good hand when she tried to assist her. "I've already been released. The papers are in the bag with my things—next appointments and such." She pointed to a clear plastic bag on the bed. "Chandler said he was selling the truck. I say good riddance." She grabbed her bag, and as she walked past Henry, she said, "I'm supposed to ring that buzzer thing so someone can take me down in a wheelchair. Wheelchair," she scoffed. "Why would I need a wheelchair? I've broken my arm, not my legs! Is he waiting in the parking lot too embarrassed to come up for me?"

Henry was surprised by the contrary tone in her friend's voice. Edee was usually positive and pleasant. Did she somehow know that something was wrong? Mothers were like that. They seemed to know things. Like when Henry fell from the hayloft and broke her arm when she was nine. Henry had barely hit the ground when her mother appeared saying she'd known something had happened to one of her girls; it had only been a matter of who and where.

"I don't know where Chandler is, Edee," Henry answered. "He didn't pick me up this morning, and he's not answering his cell."

Edee halted in the doorway but didn't turn to Henry. She stared straight ahead as a woman in scrubs pushed a man in a wheelchair by. "Has my boy gone again?" she asked, not sounding like herself. "Has he left us, Henry?"

That had not occurred to Henry until the widow spoke the words out loud. Chandler couldn't have left. They were going to get married. They would live with Edee, care for her and raise a family on the farm where he grew up. He was about to be baptized and join the church. He wouldn't leave her, leave his mother. Not now... *Would he?*

The shock of the possibility numbed Henry, and she had to will herself to Edee's side. "I don't know if he's gone," she murmured. "I don't know where he is. A friend gave me a ride, and she's going to take us back to your place."

The older woman stared straight ahead, tears glimmering in her eyes. "He wouldn't leave again without saying goodbye. He promised me," she told Henry. "He said he was staying, but I made him promise that if he ever changed his mind—" The words caught in her throat, and when she spoke again, her voice was gravelly. "If he ever left again, he promised to say goodbye."

Henry wanted to reassure Edee. She wanted to tell her all the possible reasons why Chandler hadn't shown up for them. But she held back because there were no good excuses and she didn't want to offer any additional possibilities for fear they were worse than what Edee might imagine. Instead, she put her arm around the widow, hugged her and then led her to the elevator.

Their trip to Edee's farm in Rose Valley was uneventful. Neither she nor Edee brought up Chandler on the twenty-minute ride home. Instead, they tried to chat with Rosie as if nothing was wrong. Thankfully, Rosie didn't accept Edee's offer to come inside and have a muffin and tea. Without daring to check to see if Chandler's truck was parked behind the barn, Henry escorted Edee inside, carrying the plastic bag with her belongings.

The widow sat down on a chair in the newly renovated kitchen that still smelled of fresh paint.

Henry stood in the middle of the kitchen, unsure what to do, which was unlike her. She was a woman of action who wanted answers, good or bad. But she was afraid now. She was afraid to go in search of Chandler for fear his truck was gone and they would never hear from him again. As long as she stood there, that possibility was only a probability and not a truth.

Edee pressed her knotted hands to the table. "He was upset last night. Agitated. Pacing," she said aloud. "I should have asked him what was wrong."

"Ya," Henry agreed. "He was stressed. I thought it was because he was worried about you."

Edee pursed her lips, staring but not seeing. *"Nay,* I don't think it was just about me. I could see it in his eyes."

"You think it was me? Us?" Henry looked at her. She and Edee had become close over the last few months, and the thought of being this woman's daughter-in-law had thrilled her. Now it seemed that it wouldn't come to be. "I didn't mean to pressure him. I told him time and time again that there was no hurry to marry. I told him we'd be married for the rest of our days. I told him he'd be sick of me soon enough." She reflected on the time she had said that to him. They had laughed together. It wasn't funny now.

"Ach, I doubt this is about you. He loves you, Henry."

Henry felt herself blush.

"*Nay*. It was none of those things. All of them, perhaps." Edee shook her head slowly. "Men... They're so afraid to talk about what they're thinking and feeling. Their fears. They work themselves into corners sometimes over the worry of it. Corners they don't know how to find their way out of." Edee sighed and looked up at Henry. "I suppose there's nothing to do now but look for him. I'll make tea." She rose slowly, seeming to have aged since the day before.

"You should sit and let me do it," Henry argued.

Edee ignored her. She carried the water kettle to the sink and turned on the faucet with her good hand. "Go see if the truck is still here. If it's not—" she shrugged "—we have our answer."

Henry stood there, still unable to move.

"Go on with you, now," Edee said gently. "Trust me. As a woman who lost a son and a husband to early graves, it's better to know than not, no matter the heartbreak to come."

So outside Henry went. As she walked through the barnyard, Edee's old collie at her side, she noticed that the henhouse door hadn't been opened to let the chickens into their run. Edee had done that every morning until her son returned home, and then Chandler had done it for her. Then she heard the sounds coming from the barn: the whinny of the horses, the bleat of goats and sheep. She knew that sound. She heard it most mornings when she went to her family's barn to feed up, though the cries weren't so plaintive. Those were the sounds of hungry animals.

Henry halted at the edge of a smaller barn that had been many things over the years but now stored old farm equipment. She didn't want to walk around the corner. What if the truck was gone? That would mean Chandler was gone. A lump rose in her throat. A part of her wanted to walk away. To walk down the lane and home. Edee said knowing no matter the answer was better, but was that true? Was it better to have no hope than the tiniest sliver?

But she told the widow she would check, so she would. Henry took a deep breath and strode around the corner. The white truck was there. Chandler's truck was parked where it had been for the last two months.

So where was Chandler? Surely he didn't leave home on foot. That made no sense. If he had changed his mind about staying, about her, he would have gone in his truck to return to his *Englisher* life. You had to have a motor vehicle to be an *Englisher* who worked construction. She scanned the horizon, and the dog wandered off. Henry saw fields with rows of foot-high field corn. She saw the trees surrounding the Gingerich pond in the distance, but no Chandler.

Where was he? She walked slowly back into the barnyard. Was he still in bed? Had he overslept? She almost laughed at the thought of it. Of the simple, silly explanation and her awful assumption. Had she thought Chandler had left her and his mother when his only blunder was oversleeping?

Henry didn't know if she should laugh or cry. She started to make her way back to the house to tell Edee the truck was still there when, out of the corner of her eye, she noticed that the main barn door was slightly open. She stared at it, her mind turning.

A door was never left open at night. An open barn door was dangerous. Stray dogs could get in. Last year, one of the families from her church district had a pack of stray dogs kill half their herd of sheep because a door was left ajar.

Confused, Henry walked to the door and slid it open far enough to walk inside. *"Hallo?"* she called. She glanced around and saw nothing out of order. The stall doors were closed. The feed room door was closed and secured. Yet the animals were obviously hungry. She was greeted with a frenzy of mooing, bleating and neighing. Horses thrust their heads over the stall doors and goats butted the slat walls of their stalls, trying to get her attention.

A black-and-orange barn cat rubbed against Henry's ankle, and she leaned down to pet it, still trying to figure out what was going on. Why was the barn door open and where was—

A sound caught Henry's attention. A man groaning.

"Chandler?" she called, panic rising in her chest. She took a step forward, trying to figure out where it had come from. "Chandler?" she said louder, fearing he had fallen from the hayloft or been injured somehow. Injuries, even deaths were commonplace on farms.

She heard a rustle. It came from the stall where Edee kept hay and straw so it didn't have to be brought down from the loft daily. She walked to the stall and swung open the door.

And there was Chandler, lying on his side on a pile of loose straw. His boots were off, his feet bare. "Chandler!" she repeated, shocked and afraid he was injured.

He rolled onto his back and opened his eyes, drawing his hand over his brows to block the bright sunlight. "Henry?" He squinted at her as if unsure whether she was real or a dream.

"Are you hurt?" she cried, rushing toward

him. As she stepped forward, she hit something with the toe of her sneaker, and it made a
tinny sound as it rolled away. She looked down,
startled, and saw an empty silver-and-blue can.
There were cans all over the floor. All empty.
She smelled something stale and yeasty. And
then she knew what had been in the cans.

Beer.

Sunlight streamed into the stall, nearly blind-
ing Chandler, and he blinked in confusion.
Through the haze of dust motes, he saw a figure. She spoke his name.

Henry. It was his Henry. His smart, capable,
beautiful betrothed.

But why was she looking at him like that?
He glanced around, trying to get his bearings.
Why was he lying in an itchy bed of straw?

He drew his hand across his face, foggy
memories flitting past him. He was thirsty, and
his mouth was dry. His head pounded, and he
felt slightly nauseated, a feeling he vaguely remembered from his past. As his head cleared
slightly, he felt like he was on the verge of understanding what was happening here.

Then he heard a familiar tinny clink…fol-
lowed by a more forceful one. A beer can flew
up into the air and almost clipped his ear as it
went by. She had kicked it at him.

"You've been drinking alcohol!" Henry accused. "Your poor mother was waiting for you at the hospital, and you were out here drinking?" she demanded.

He sat up, resisting the urge to cover his ears to block out her piercing voice. "Henry…" He exhaled and licked his lips. Now the memories were flooding him, sharp and ugly. "I wasn't drinking this morning. I had a few beers last night. I guess I fell asleep."

She kicked another can at him. This one went over his head, missing him by inches.

"How could you do this to her? To us?" She hesitated. "Chandler, how could you do this to yourself?"

She spun around to go, and he leaped up. "Henry, wait."

He was in the stall doorway when she turned back to him, her hands on her hips. Her face was pale with bright red spots on her cheeks.

"I don't know what to say to you, Chandler." She didn't raise her voice now, but there was no doubting the severity of her anger. "You told me you used to drink alcohol, but that you stopped. You said that you were *sober*."

He hung his head feeling as if the world were crashing down on him. His stomach churned, and he felt weak in his legs. "I'm sorry," he whispered. "I… I don't know what happened.

I was driving home, and I saw a liquor store, and I guess I—" He covered his eyes with his hand, willing himself not to cry. How could he have done something so stupid? How could he have done this to Henry? He didn't deserve her. She was too good for him. Too perfect.

"You guess what?" she demanded. "Why would you do this when things were going so well?" Her voice trembled. "I don't understand."

He didn't, either. How could he explain to her what he didn't understand himself? He exhaled. "I don't know what happened." He pressed the heel of his hand to his pounding head. "I went into the store and bought a twelve-pack, and I guess... I came to the barn because this is a place where I've always felt...safe." He raised his arms and let them fall to his sides. "I guess I drank it all."

She said nothing, and he lifted his head to meet her gaze. There were tears in her eyes.

"Your mother deserves better than this, Chandler." She gestured wildly toward the house, then brought her hand to her chest. "And I don't deserve this, either."

"I'm sorry." He took a shuddering breath, wishing for the world to stop spinning. "I was upset."

"And you think the rest of us don't get upset

sometimes?" she demanded. "We do, but we don't do…that." She pointed at the cans that littered the stall. "That's not how we handle our worries. That's not how we do it here."

He looked past her into the barnyard through the opening of the sliding door. "Maybe I can't do this," he said quietly. "It was foolish of me to think I could. To ever think I could come home."

He met her gaze again. "I release you, Henry. I release you from our agreement to—" He almost couldn't get the last words out. He was so ashamed. So embarrassed by his actions. "From our agreement to wed. I'll never be the man you want me to be. The man you deserve." He looked down at his bare feet. "Sam is a better man than I am. You should go back to Sam, Henry. Marry him."

"Don't tell me what to do," she shouted at him. "I don't want Sam, I want—" She halted midsentence and stared at him. Then she walked away, leaving Chandler with the greatest sense of hopelessness he had ever felt.

Chapter Thirteen

Henry slid a pine board onto the brackets she'd set in the store's storage room wall and groaned aloud. It was too short, and this was the second time she'd made a mistake. She couldn't concentrate on anything, which wasn't like her. It had been that way for more than a week now. She'd felt scattered and a bit lost since she'd hugged Edee tightly and promised to get in touch when she was ready to talk.

Henry hadn't told Edee that day why Chandler hadn't come to the hospital to pick her up. All she said was that she had found him in the barn, he was safe and they had broken up. Tears had filled Edee's eyes, and Henry's too as they hugged. Thankfully, the widow hadn't pressed for details, and Henry didn't offer them. It wasn't her place to tell Chandler's mother what he had done. It was his.

In the days since then, Henry had spent hour upon hour going over in her mind what she could have done to prevent the ruination of the life with Chandler she had dreamed of. She vacillated between setting the blame for Chandler's inexcusable actions directly on his shoulders and wondering if it was, somehow, her fault. Sometimes she was angry; sometimes she was sad. Sometimes she was both at the same time, and she didn't know what to do with those feelings. She wondered if she had been wrong to choose Chandler over Sam. Had it been a mistake from the beginning to have thought a man who had left his faith could find it again? She told herself she shouldn't have allowed herself to fall in love with him. What had her love for him gotten her but a broken heart? Sam would never break her heart because she never would give it to him.

When Henry arrived home that day after catching a ride with a neighbor, she told her sisters what had happened because there was no keeping secrets from them. Then she'd asked them not to bring up the topic again. Of course, that request had been in vain. Since then, it seemed as if the Koffman women had talked about nothing *but* her breakup and about what Chandler had done. Everyone had opinions and suggestions. Some of her sisters thought she had made the right choice to walk away, others thought maybe she had been too quick to end her relationship with him. Sometimes they switched positions in the same conversation. But Henry refused to hear anything they said. It was over. For all she knew, Chandler was already gone, headed back to Illinois and his *Englisher* life.

"I said that's too short," Henry's father declared, tapping the board she held in her hand and breaking Henry from her thoughts.

She glanced at him. He was arranging her tools on a makeshift worktable in some order that only made sense to him. He wasn't having a good day. Since he'd risen that morning, he'd been quiet and often confused. He kept trying to leave the property, thinking he had to be at an auction to buy a new plow. Hoping to keep her mind off Chandler, she had offered to keep him with her, even though Eleanor had given her a long list of tasks to do at the store. She and her father had already snaked out her sister Beth's kitchen sink in the apartment above the store, put a deadbolt on the back door, shimmed up two sets of metal shelving for a flea-and-tick product display and put in a new mailbox out on the road after someone had run into their old one with a car or truck.

"Cut it and cut it and it's still too short," her *dat* murmured as he turned a nail set over with his fingers, obviously trying to identify what it was. He was the one who had taught her how to use a nail set to sink the head of a finishing nail below the surface of the wood. The one he had plucked from her toolbox had been his.

She smiled at him, but it was a sad smile. Seeing him like this was hard, especially after he'd had several good days in a row. Sometimes he was his old self, and anyone who didn't know him wouldn't realize he had dementia. The only good thing about him being in this state today was that he hadn't asked her when she and Chandler were getting married. Today, he didn't remember that she had been the happiest woman in Honeycomb for a few weeks.

"You hear me?" he asked.

"I heard you, *Dat*. You're right. I cut another one too short." She shook her head. "I don't know what's wrong with me today. I keep making silly mistakes."

"You're making mistakes because you're all long-faced and grumpy."

She knit her brows and reached out to adjust his worn leather suspenders. "I'm not being *grumpy*. I haven't been grumpy with you." *I hope I haven't*, she thought. In her mind, caring for her father in his state was a gift. It was always a gift from *Gott* to be able to help another. Her *mam* had taught her that.

He plopped down on a step stool. They

needed more space to stockpile their inventory and get cardboard boxes off the floor. The store had prospered beyond their wildest dreams in the year since they'd opened it. Not only had *Gott* provided them with the finances they needed to care for their farm and their father's growing medical bills, but they had been blessed with enough to start helping other folks again.

While the Amish paid income taxes, they didn't receive social security, welfare, unemployment benefits or participate in any health insurance plans. That meant that church districts financially supported their members in need, and with the new windfall, the Felty Koffmans had been able to help several families in the last few months, including Eleanor's recently departed friend Sara's.

Henry set the wrong-sized board aside for something else and grabbed the next one she'd cut, hoping it would be right. "What did I say to you that made you think I was grumpy?" she asked, purposely leaving out his comment about her looking sad. It was interesting that he could no longer tie his shoes, but he was more aware of the emotions of others than he had once been. More empathetic. It was as if as one part of his brain began to shut down, another had flourished.

"You were grumpy with your sisters," he accused. "Willa came in, sweet as you please, asking if you wanted a glass of tea, and you nearly bit her head off."

"I did not—" Henry caught herself midsentence and took a deep breath before she went on. "I didn't bite her head off. It was the third or fourth time she'd offered, *Dat*, in an hour." She set the board down, wondering if she ought to find something else to do and leave the shelves for another day when she could hopefully focus better. "She's fussing over me. They all are. They're smothering me." Henry held up her hands. "I don't want to be smothered. I just want to be left alone."

"Then you should have been born into another family," he told her. "They're worried about you, is all." He frowned and stroked his beard, which had turned entirely gray since their mother died. "Why are we worried?"

Henry pressed her lips together, willing her eyes not to tear up. "I'm fine, *Dat*. Just a little... heartbreak is all," she said, choking up.

"Ah, that boy Sam." He waggled his finger at her. "It's just as well you two broke up. I didn't think Sam was right for you. Your mother and I talked about it. I wanted to tell you so ages ago, but she said when it comes to our daughters, I should mind my own knitting."

He chuckled, and it tugged at her heartstrings. Their mother had passed away three years ago, but they rarely reminded him of that anymore. What was the sense in it? He'd forget, and then there would be the pain of the memory of her death all over again.

"It wasn't Sam, *Dat*. I had another beau," Henry told him. "Chandler Gingerich from Rose Valley."

As she spoke the words, her sister Jane walked by the door, then backed up. She was carrying a large cardboard box. "What did you say about Sam? Are you going to invite him to supper like Cora suggested? She thinks he's still in love with you. Willa says he'd have you back in a second. Said you could do worse."

Henry rolled her eyes. "No one said anything about inviting Sam to supper. We broke up, remember?"

"And now you've broken up with Chandler," Jane pointed out.

"That's not exactly what happened, but fine," Henry said. "It doesn't matter how it happened. It's done. Over with." Her words were to remind herself as much as Jane. She needed to stop obsessing over Chandler. The whys and hows didn't matter. It was over, and she needed to accept that and continue her life.

Jane hugged the cardboard box to her chest,

seeming to consider whether to speak again. Henry wished she wouldn't, but that wouldn't happen with Jane. Jane was like Eleanor and their mother, never afraid to initiate a difficult conversation. "I know you don't want to hear this—"

"Then maybe don't say it," Henry murmured, feeling tears well in her eyes again.

"But I think you should talk to Chandler," Jane went on, talking over her. "If nothing else, then to clear the air. I know Edee would appreciate it, too. Eleanor says it's called closure."

"You've all been talking about me behind my back?"

"Nothing we haven't said directly to you. But of course we've been talking about you. We love you, Henry. We don't want to see you so sad. And when one of us is hurting, we all hurt."

Henry nodded in understanding.

"Anyway, I know you're angry," Jane continued, setting the box on the hallway floor. "But we're worried about Chandler, too. He must be in a terrible way. I can't imagine doing something like that and then losing your true love because of it. I can't imagine—"

"Henry!" Willa sang from out front, where she was running the cash register. "Someone here to see you!"

Henry froze. Was it Chandler? It couldn't be,

not after a week. In the first hours after she left his place, in the first days, she had hoped he would come. She had hoped that with emotions not running so high, they would sit down together and he would explain why he had done what he had done. She had hoped he would help her to understand so that even if their relationship couldn't be mended, at least she would know.

But he didn't come. And after three days of wishing she hadn't been so impulsive in walking away from him rather than demanding answers, she realized it had been better that way. Because he must not have loved her, otherwise, he'd have explained why he went into that store in the first place. He would have explained why he bought the beer and why he sat in the barn and drank it all. He'd have explained why he wanted her to go back to Sam. Which, of course, was never going to happen.

"Henry!" Willa shouted.

Jane leaned forward, her eyes wide. She loved any sort of drama in their lives. She wasn't old enough yet to understand the comfort of the mundane. "You think it's Chandler?" she whispered.

Henry sighed. *"Nay."*

"Sam, then?"

Henry scowled. "Why would Sam be looking for me?" She removed the leather apron she wore to protect her dress. "It's probably someone looking to have repairs done, which is *goot*." She left the storage room, handing her sister her leather apron. "I need to get back to work." As she walked away, she called, "Stay with Jane, *Dat*. I'll be right back."

Henry walked out onto the sales floor of the general store not to find an Amish widow, but Sam. When she spotted him at the cash register paying for a bag of cookies, she was tempted to turn and go the other way. She knew why he was here but couldn't believe he'd shown up so soon. That day at the barn raising, he said he would have her back if things didn't work out with his friend. Now he was here to make good on his promise.

"There you are," Willa called, sounding overly cheerful. "I told Sam you were working, but I was sure you'd want to see him."

Henry scowled at her sister, annoyed she had told Sam such a thing, annoyed with him for coming, annoyed with the world. "Not at work on a Tuesday morning?" she asked Sam.

He stuffed his change into his pocket and walked toward Henry, opening the bag of homemade cookies. *"Guder mariye,"* he greeted. "We got off early. Problem with the skid steer." He offered her the bag. "Want one?"

She shook her head. It was overly warm in the store, even with open windows. "Want to go outside?" she asked, not wanting an audience. Besides Jane, her *dat* and Willa, Beth and Millie were both in the kitchen cooking. It was chicken and dumpling day at the Koffman General Store, and they always sold as many quarts as they made. If she talked with Sam in the store, they would all be hanging on every word.

"Let us know if you need anything," Jane called happily.

When Henry looked back at her, she was standing with their father, grinning excitedly. Henry walked out the door and onto the front porch with Sam.

He took a big bite of a cookie. "Mmm." He looked into the bag, chewing. "White chocolate chip with macadamia nuts. They're really good. You sure you don't want one?"

"Danki, nay," she said in a hurry to get this over with.

"You're missing something mighty good," he warned her. "Anyway, I came by to—"

"I know why you came by, Sam," she interrupted. "And the answer is no. I'll not walk out with you. I won't go anywhere with you. I'm not marrying you."

He took another bite, not seeming upset by

her words. "That's not why I came, Henny. I'm seeing Elsa Troyer over in Hickory Grove. I thought you knew that."

Henry closed her eyes for a moment, embarrassed and relieved at the same time. "Sorry," she managed, looking up at him. "I'm glad to hear that you've found someone. I hadn't heard."

"Thanks." He dug another cookie from the bag. "She's not as pretty as you, but she likes me more than you did."

She stared at him, unsure how to respond, then realized he was teasing her. She laughed. "Good one."

He shrugged and began to consume the next cookie. "I came because my *mam* ran into Edee Gingerich at Byler's."

"And told her that Chandler and I had broken up, I suppose?"

"*Nay.* Everyone in the county already knew that, Henny. My *mam* and sisters call it the Amish telegraph. Good or bad news travels fast."

Henry's relief and embarrassment had passed, and now she was just eager to get back to the storeroom to fix the mess she was making of the shelving. She crossed her arms. "What did Edee tell your *mam*?"

"Mostly that Chandler got drunk, and that's

why you broke up, and that he's in a bad way. He doesn't want to see anyone. Talk to anyone. He turned the bishop away and me, too. But Edee told my *mam* that Chandler told the bishop he had no excuse for what he had done and wasn't going to talk about it."

"So, Chandler didn't leave Delaware?" she murmured, surprised. Why would he stay? Hadn't he made the choice not to join the church when he drank that beer?

Sam licked his fingers. "Not unless he left today. I stopped by his place last night, but his *mam* couldn't get him to come to the door. I came by here because I wondered if you'd tried to see him."

"Me?" She stepped back. "Why would I go? He made his choice when he did what he did."

Sam knit his bushy eyebrows. "Where's your compassion, Henry? My *dat*'s been reading from the Book of Matthew evenings during family prayer. He's been talking about having compassion for others. For forgiving others. In forgiving others, we receive forgiveness from *Gott*." He continued, "Chandler made a mistake, Henny. A bad one. But we all make mistakes. The world is full of temptations. They're meant to lead us astray."

His words made her feel very small and selfish, and she didn't know how to respond.

Sam finished the last cookie and said, "Would you want to try talking to Chandler? I could take you. Maybe he'd talk to you even if he won't talk to me."

Tears welled in Henry's eyes, and she turned away so he wouldn't see them. *Had* she been callous? Probably. She'd been so hurt by what happened. But maybe she'd seen the whole thing in the wrong way. She had seen Chandler's misstep as if she was the wounded one, but hadn't Chandler hurt *himself* the most? Now, she was ashamed.

"I can't go with you," she told him, not making eye contact.

"No?"

"Nay."

"Why not?" Sam asked.

"Because what's done is done. It's over between me and Chandler."

"You're sure?" he pressed.

She crossed her arms protectively. "I'm sure."

He stared at her momentarily, then shook his head as he went down the porch steps. "You Koffman girls sure are stubborn."

Chandler was behind the chicken coop chopping wood when he heard buggy wheels in their lane. The wood cookstove had been removed when they did the renovation. His *mam* wouldn't need wood until winter and then only for the parlor fireplace, which was more for comfort than to heat the whole house. He was chopping wood to keep himself busy, to tire himself out so he would hopefully sleep that night finally. And in case tomorrow was the day he decided to leave.

Every night, he went to bed thinking the next day would be the day he left. But he realized that he hadn't left because he had nowhere to go, nothing to go *to*. All there was in Illinois, or any other state for that matter, was a carpentry job like any other job and a rented place he'd share with other guys. He had no one anywhere but here.

Chandler couldn't believe he had been so stupid as to have stopped for that beer in the first place. He hadn't done that once since he'd quit. How could he not have seen that walking into that liquor store would reverse everything good that had happened in the last two months? Had he not realized that buying that beer would ruin his relationship with his mother, his community and Henry?

He couldn't even think about Henry. He missed her so much that it hurt. He missed her laughter, teasing and even how she held a hammer. He missed the life they had talked about building together. A life that would never come to be now.

Chandler heard the buggy stop at the hitching post, then the sound of boots hitting the ground. *Who's come to see the man fallen from grace now?* he wondered irritably.

A parade of folks, mostly men, had been rolling up and down the driveway for a week. Bishop Cyrus had come twice, three preachers, two from Honeycomb, the other from his mother's church district here in Rose Valley. Everyone wanted to talk to him, to help him, but he didn't want anyone's help. It didn't matter who it was. His mother would send them away as she had sent the others at his behest.

Chandler split another log. He wondered where Henry was today. What she was doing. Was she thinking of him? He hoped she was because that would mean she had truly loved him, at least briefly. But then he decided he hoped she wasn't because he didn't want to cause her more pain than he already had.

A few minutes later, as Chandler set the axe aside and began to stack the wood he'd cut, he heard his mother's voice and the low rumble of a male voice. He groaned. He'd been very clear that he was not interested in talking to anyone. Not even the bishop. Who was she leading through the barnyard and straight for him?

"Help yourself," he heard his mother say from the other side of the chicken coop. "I can't do a thing with him."

Chandler didn't look up when the man walked to the back of the henhouse. Instead, he lifted the axe and swung it hard. He swung it angrily because he was angry at himself. He didn't know what to do. How to start his life again.

"Chandler."

He looked up, then lowered his head and swung the axe again. It was Sam. His buddy was persistent, he'd give him that. This was the fourth time he'd been there in the last week. "I've got nothing to say to you."

"*Goot*. Because I didn't come to hear anything you have to say," Sam responded in a direct tone that surprised Chandler. It wasn't like Sam to speak with such conviction.

"You didn't?" Chandler lowered his axe, confused.

"I came to tell you something. Some things," Sam amended.

"Okay." Chandler drew out the word, perplexed.

"Okay," Sam repeated. "I wanted to say that you're not the first man to have made a mistake. To have sinned." He began to pace, head down as if he had rehearsed his words and wanted to be sure to get them right. "King David, the Apostle Paul, the prodigal son. They all sinned and were forgiven for their sins because they wanted forgiveness." He glanced at Chandler. "What makes you think you're different?"

"What?" Chandler asked.

"What makes you think you're different from those men in the Bible? You're no better but no worse," Sam told him. "You did something you shouldn't have. I don't know why. But I'm guessing that you don't want to talk to anyone who cares about you. Because you think you can't be forgiven, and that's wrong." He shook his head. "*You're* wrong, and for you to think that God can't forgive you isn't seeing Him as He is. He's all-powerful, Chandler. But you have to want it. You must want His forgiveness." He pointed his finger at his friend. "You have to *want* to never drink alcohol again. You have to *want* to be baptized. You have to *want* to be saved."

Chandler was overwhelmed by his friend's words. He was so overcome by the sudden realization of the truth of what Sam said that it took him a moment to realize that his buddy was no longer speaking.

When Chandler met Sam's gaze, Sam said, "Do you want to be forgiven by *Gott*?"

Chandler nodded slowly. "I do," he said, his words catching in his throat.

"*Goot.* Then let's go."

"Go where?" Chandler asked.

"Change your clothes." Sam scowled at Chandler's jeans and ripped T-shirt. "We're going to Bishop Cyrus. He'll know what to do. How to get you on the right path again."

"Now?" Chandler asked in disbelief.

"Now," Sam agreed, striding off. "I'll wait for you in the buggy. We're going to the bishop's and then making another stop."

"Where?" Chandler called to his back.

"Guess you'll just have to wait and see."

Chapter Fourteen

That afternoon, Chandler climbed into Sam's fancy buggy in the bishop's barnyard. His friend was leaning back in the leather seat, his straw hat pulled down to cover his face. Sam didn't move when Chandler sat down and slid the door closed.

Was Sam napping? Chandler had been inside Bishop Cyrus's house for two hours, so it was possible. Or, from the look of the discarded chip and candy wrappers on the floor, maybe he was in what the *English* guys called a food coma.

Chandler wasn't sure what to do. He leaned back against the seat and sighed. He had shown up on the bishop's porch feeling lost and defeated but now everything seemed lighter and brighter. After talking for a long time, he and the bishop prayed together, and with those prayers, Chandler felt hope again. He felt confident that he could follow the plan he and the spiritual leader had mapped out for the coming days and weeks.

"*Goot* visit?" Sam asked from beneath his hat.

Chandler turned to his buddy, grinning. "*Ya.* Thank you for bringing me and for waiting. I don't know if I would have come on my own. *Danki* for not giving up on me when I'd given up on myself."

"You'd do the same for me, wouldn't you?" Sam questioned, his face still covered by his hat.

Chandler thought for a moment. "I think so." He nodded, now feeling certain in his answer. "*Ya*, I would. I would do that for you, Sam. I'd do anything for you."

"You talk to the bishop about getting baptized?"

"I did. I'll start counseling again, and when he thinks I'm ready, we'll set a date. He says he thinks things will be easier for me once I truly commit."

"*Goot.*" Sam pushed his hat back onto his head, dropped his feet to the floorboards and kicked a discarded mini doughnut package out of the way. He reached for the reins tied on the handbrake. "Next stop, Koffman's store."

Chandler stared at the trash on the floor. "Need more snacks, do you?"

"Nay." Sam made a clicking sound to catch his driving horse's attention and eased the buggy down the driveway.

"Then why—" Chandler suddenly realized why they were going to the Koffmans'. "Oh, no." He shook his head. *"Nay*, I'm not ready. I can't face her yet."

"I know she can be scary," Sam said. "But you can face her."

"No," Chandler repeated. "Look, I know I need to talk to her. To try to explain what happened. I have a better understanding now that I talked to Bishop Cyrus. He's counseled other men with a drinking problem. He said nothing I did was uncommon. But… I need some time. I need to think about what to say to her." He turned to his friend. "And why would you help me try to patch things up with Henry? She was your girl before she was mine."

Sam shrugged. "Because you two belong together. So we're going. Putting it off isn't going to make that any easier. And the longer you wait, the more you hurt that girl." He halted the buggy at the end of the lane. "I think she'll be glad to see you. But if she isn't, why not get it over with?"

Chandler pressed his hand to his chest. His heart pounded, and he was finding it harder to breathe. Bishop Cyrus said that when he started feeling like this, as he had that night in the hospital, it was a panic attack coming on. He gave him suggestions on how to keep it from worsening, and even stop it. So Chandler sat back and closed his eyes and breathed deeply. As he tried to will his heart to calm, he felt the buggy roll forward, and they turned to the right. Left was home in Rose Valley. Right was the Koffman farm.

So as he continued to breathe, he resigned himself to the idea of facing Henry. He reminded himself of the connection they'd had before he'd fallen off the wagon. Of the love that had been blossoming between them. And by the time they pulled into the store parking lot, he was excited to see her.

He wasn't convinced she would feel the same way.

Henry hung a hummingbird feeder on an iron shepherd's hook in the flower bed in front of the store. As she leaned down to pick up the packaging, she spotted Sam's buggy on the main road, waiting for a car to pass before turning in. Even at this distance, she saw two men in the front seat and immediately recognized the passenger.

Her first impulse was to run. To kick off her sneakers and run as far away as possible. But she wasn't a coward. She wasn't one to hide from her problems. And right now, Chandler Gingerich was a problem. So, like it or not, the logical thing to do was to hear him out and bring the closure Jane spoke of to their relationship.

But life wasn't always logical. And love, she realized as she watched Chandler step tentatively out of Sam's buggy, certainly wasn't logical. Maybe that was what made it so glorious. So scary but wonderful in the same heartbeat.

Since Henry had last seen Chandler, she'd rehearsed over and over in her head what she would say to him if she ever spoke to him again. She would tell him how terrible he had been, how he had ruined everything. Those words, if not mean, she realized now, were uncharitable. They were not the things a woman said to the man she loved. Not even to the man she had loved and lost.

Chandler was halfway across the parking lot before he dared to meet her gaze. He stopped and stared. He wore the same clothing as every Amish man in Honeycomb: homemade trousers and shirt, a straw hat and suspenders. But he wasn't any other man. He was the man she loved, and even though he had done that terrible thing and disappointed and hurt her, she suddenly realized that she still loved him. She wanted to be with him. She wanted to help him through his crisis of faith and see him to the end, wherever that end was.

Henry started to run. Toward him. His expression went from shock to disbelief as she grew closer, then he was running, too.

"I'm sorry," Henry cried as she ran into his open arms. "I'm sorry for being so selfish," she gushed. "For thinking of myself and not you. For not staying and fighting for us instead of walking away."

"Shh," he hushed, pulling her close. "It's all right, my *liebchen*."

"But it's not all right," she argued, looking up at him. Tears trickled down her cheeks. "I abandoned you when you needed me the most."

"It doesn't matter," he told her. "None of that matters now. Only this," he said, pulling her close and gazing into her eyes.

A sound of applause came from the store's front porch, and Henry turned around in surprise to see all her sisters and her *dat* standing at the rail, clapping. Henry giggled with embarrassment and joy, resting her head on Chandler's shoulder for a moment. He felt so good that she could have stood there in his arms for the remaining days of her life. But then she realized that not only was her family witnessing her inappropriate behavior, but Sam was watching it all, too.

"Oh," she said, stepping out of Chandler's arms but letting him hold her hand.

He grinned, then leaned close and murmured, "While I'd like to keep that up a while longer, we need to talk."

She laughed and used the corner of her apron to wipe the tears of happiness from her eyes. "*Ya*, we do. Want to go for a walk?" She glanced at her sisters, still standing at the rail. Jane waved wildly, bouncing on the balls of her bare feet as if she were still a child. "Otherwise," she said, looking up at him, "we'll have an audience."

"A walk sounds like a good idea." He turned to Sam's buggy and raised his hand. *"Danki,"* he called. "I'll make my way home on my own."

Henry looked across the parking lot to see Sam watching them. "Thank you," she called, her chest tight with emotion. Sam would never be the right man for her, but he was a good friend.

Sam waved to them both as he pulled out in his buggy.

Henry tugged on Chandler's hand. "Come on. Let's this go this way."

Jane leaned over the rail as they walked past her family, who were finally scattering to go about their business. "Want to join us for supper, Chandler?" she called. "We made chicken and dumplings! There'll be buttermilk biscuits, lima beans and chowchow. And strawberry-rhubarb pie for dessert!"

Chandler glanced at Henry, then called to Jane, "We'll have to see how your sister feels about that. Can I hold off a bit before accepting the invitation?"

"She better say yes!" Jane said, laughing. "To all your questions. And if she doesn't say yes to marrying you, I will!"

Henry's eyes grew wide in astonishment as Chandler laughed heartily. Walking past the store, Henry saw Eleanor grab their little sister and lead her inside, chastising her as they went.

Henry couldn't stop giggling as she and Chandler walked across the grass toward the wooded portion of their property. "I can't believe she said such a thing." She pressed her free hand to her face. "I'm embarrassed for myself and for her. I don't know where she got her brazenness. Our mother must be rolling over in her grave."

"Don't be embarrassed. You're refreshing, you Koffman women. She's young and full of life. She doesn't actually want to marry me."

Henry pressed her lips together, trying to suppress another fit of giggles. "*Nay*, I think she's completely serious," she told him as she led him onto a well-worn path at the edge of the woods.

"Well then, I'm sorry I'll have to disappoint her." He stopped and pressed her hand to his chest. "Because if I have my way, you're the woman I want to call wife."

She smiled up at him, unable to believe how this was all unfolding. That morning, she'd woken up feeling as if the world were about to end, and now she saw nothing but hope and promise.

"But first, we have to talk," Chandler said, growing serious. "I've been to see Bishop Cyrus."

"You have?" she asked, leading him farther into the cool forest.

"I have, but not of my own wishes. At least it wasn't my idea. It was Sam's," he explained. "He came to see me again and wouldn't take no for an answer. He's the one who finally talked some sense into me. He practically kidnapped me and took me to your uncle's house."

"Sam did that? Our Sam?" she asked in disbelief.

"I know. Hard to believe. I didn't know he had it in him. But sometimes people surprise us. Don't they?" He glanced around. "Where are you taking me?"

"It's only a little farther. I want to show you the first thing I ever built. And Janey won't think to look for us here," she teased.

They followed the deer path around a cluster of large gum trees, and she pointed. "There it is," she said, pointing to the plank structure built from scrap wood in the crook of a massive silver maple.

"A treehouse?" he exclaimed. He released her hand to walk around one side and then the other.

The floor was just above Henry's head now, but when she'd built it, it seemed like a tower in the trees. "I built it myself. I was ten."

"Doesn't surprise me." He nodded approvingly. "Built well, especially for a ten-year-old," he said over his shoulder. "Is it safe to go up?"

"Of course, it's safe," she scoffed. "I make repairs every year."

"I shouldn't be surprised," he told her, pride in his voice.

She was self-conscious and pleased at the same time by his complimentary tone, and she pointed at the ladder built from small lengths of board nailed to the tree trunk. "You first." She gestured upward.

Chandler climbed up into the treehouse, and Henry followed. While the sturdy structure had a roof, there were no walls, so they sat on the far side of the platform and dangled their feet off the edge. Henry kicked off her sneakers as she had done when she was ten, then turned to him. "Time for that talk," she said quietly.

"Ya." He took her hand, squeezed it and gazed out from their perch in the trees. "When you found me that morning, Henry, I told you I didn't know why I did what I did. I'm sorry I didn't give you a better answer. I was embarrassed and so angry at myself and..." He looked at her. "I honestly didn't understand why I had done it, but after talking to your uncle, it all makes sense to me now." He shrugged. "I was overwhelmed. I was scared. When I returned to Delaware, I thought I was only coming back to see my mother for a couple of weeks."

She squeezed his hand, feeling his pain.

"But looking back, I don't know that that's true. I didn't leave Illinois like a man expecting to return. I paid my rent to the end of my lease, took my savings and closed my bank account. So even though I didn't know I wanted to be Amish again, I think subconsciously I did." He knit his brow. "Does that make sense?"

She nodded but said nothing.

"So, on some level, I think I *did* want to return to the church. And then I met you, and... and things started falling into place. But then

I began to feel pressure. I got scared. Overwhelmed."

"I'm sorry," Henry said, her heart aching for him. She couldn't believe that she had been so self-centered, so wrapped up in the idea of romance, that she hadn't been paying attention to what was happening with the man she loved. "I didn't mean to pressure you."

"You didn't do that. I pressured myself," he told her. "You were honest with me. You told me that you wouldn't leave the church. I decided I wanted to be a part of it to be with you. But I also realized that I needed the church. With or without you."

She nodded, trying to take in everything he was saying, trying to understand it.

"But then my sessions with Bishop Cyrus were starting to get intense. I started attending church, you and I were discussing getting married, *Mam* was making plans for you and me to live with her, and I... I started to worry that I wasn't up to the task. I was afraid I couldn't be the man I wanted to be for all of you. For *Gott*. For myself."

He was quiet for a moment, then went on. "And then *Mam* got hurt and—" He lifted his hand and let it fall. "I slipped. I forgot that the booze never helps and only makes things worse, and in a moment of weakness, I bought the beer. And I drank it."

"I wish I'd known how upset you were that night," Henry murmured. "I should have known."

"And I should have been man enough to tell you." He took a deep breath and exhaled. "Bishop Cyrus says this sometimes happens with alcoholics. I think I was one. Am. Although I never admitted that to myself. He says it happens but promises me that doesn't mean it'll happen again. He says that I'll always have to stay vigilant. I'll have to continue to meet with him or others like him for the rest of my life. But with the help of the church, our community and God, he says I can stay sober." He looked down at her. "You know what else your uncle told me?"

"What?" she whispered, holding his hand tightly.

"He said he thinks I can be the man I want to be with you at my side. So, before I ask you to marry me, Henry, I have to ask if you're willing to help me be a man we can both be proud of."

She turned to him and threw her arms around his neck. "Yes, yes, yes," she told him. "Because I love you and want to spend the rest of my life with you."

"Guess it works out for the both of us, then,"

he teased. "Because I love you, Henry Koffman. And I want to spend the rest of my life with you," he whispered in her ear.

Chandler pressed a kiss to her cheek, and Henry knew that he was the man God had always intended to be her husband. She knew he would be the man he wanted to be for her, his mother and his community, and that their life together would be a happy one.

Epilogue

Two years later,
Kent County, Delaware

After washing up for supper, Chandler walked into the kitchen and inhaled the heavenly scent of just-baked buttermilk biscuits. "Mmm, smells *goot*," he told his mother. "I'm starving."

She turned from the stove, a wooden spoon in her hand. "We'll be ready to eat in five minutes." She pursed her lips in amusement. "Though we're missing one thing."

"What's that?"

"My daughter-in-law?"

He glanced in the direction of the door, then back at her. "She never came in?"

His mother lifted her brows. "Where is she? I called you in half an hour ago."

He smiled, shaking his head. "I'll be back in a minute. With my wife."

"Don't dally," she warned as he left the

kitchen. "I'm about to mash the potatoes, and the chicken-fried steak is already done."

"Be right in. I promise."

"That's what you two always say," she called after him good-naturedly. For all her fussing with them, Chandler knew that his *mam* loved having him home, and maybe loved that Henry was now part of their family even more.

Smiling, he walked out of the house and their year-old collie, which had replaced his mother's old dog that had passed, fell into step beside him. "Hey, girl," he greeted, giving her a pat on the head. "I suppose you know where our Henry is, don't you?"

At the sound of his wife's name, the dog shot forward, leading the way, and Chandler followed. He crossed the barnyard and walked through the new orchard they had planted and into view of the one-story *grossmammi haus* they were building for his mother. It had been his *mam*'s idea. He and Henry had agreed that when they married, there was no reason they couldn't share the same home; many families lived in multigenerational homes. While it was not overly large, there was plenty of room in the house, but his *mudder* had been insistent. She told them she didn't like climbing stairs anymore, but they knew it was her way of wanting to give the newlyweds privacy.

Chandler scanned the worksite. "Henry?" he called.

"Here!" she answered.

He looked around but didn't see her.

Her laughter rang out in the cool spring air. "Up here, husband!"

Chandler looked up to see his pretty wife sitting on the roof's ridgeline, dressed in her work pants and one of his shirts. She waved, grinning at him.

"What are you doing up there?" he demanded, walking toward the ladder that leaned against the nearly completed house.

She didn't answer until he had climbed the ladder and crossed the roof to sit beside her. "What am I doing up here? Just taking in the view," she told him with a smile of contentment. "Join me."

"*Mam* sent me to fetch you. She's about to put supper on the table."

She patted the spot beside her. "Just for a minute. It's so beautiful," she told him, gazing over the rooftops. "I want to enjoy it with you, husband."

He wanted to protest but knew from experience that the quickest way to get his stubborn wife off the roof was to go along with her wishes. He sat down beside her and slid his arm around her shoulders. Gazing out at their neighbor's freshly tilled field, he was filled with gladness.

It was still hard for Chandler to believe he could be this happy. All those years he spent trying to find himself in the *Englisher* world now felt like a hazy dream. He regretted wasting so many years of his life searching for the very things he had left behind.

It was Henry who convinced him that maybe he had needed to leave his community and church to appreciate how much he belonged here. Once he committed to the baptism and asked Henry Koffman to marry him, everything fell into place. He had attended the bishop's counseling sessions for his religious studies and continued to remain sober. He had not had a sip of alcohol since the morning Henry found him hungover in the barn. Forgiving himself for that misstep had taken a while, but with Henry's help, he had managed to set that guilt aside. Now, instead of waking to regrets every morning, he woke to his wife's beautiful face and the joy his life in the church and community brought to their lives. Just thinking about it made him misty-eyed.

But there was no time for sentiments because he needed to get his wife off this roof. He glanced at her, thinking about his word choice before speaking because if there was one thing he knew about Henry, it was that she was independent-minded. "Do you think it's wise to be up here?" he asked.

She glanced at him, a twinkle in her blue eyes. "Why not? I'm not afraid of heights anymore. Putting on this roof with you fixed that." She gazed out over the farm again. "Now I like it up here. I like seeing our cows, the horses and our clothes flapping on the line."

"But *should* you be up here?" he pressed. "In your condition?" She laughed. "What's so funny?" he asked.

"You." She poked him in the chest with her finger. "This *boppli* is only the size of a lima bean," she murmured in his ear.

He wanted to press her further, but decided it would be better to have this conversation later, preferably when they weren't sitting on a roof. He changed topics. "We'd best go anyway. *Mam*'s made chicken-fried steak *and* biscuits and won't be happy if her mashed potatoes get cold."

"Oll recht."

She went to stand, and Chandler grabbed her hand. "Will you let me help you down?"

"I don't need help, husband," she said, remaining seated.

"I know you don't," he answered quietly, emotion thick in his throat. "But I want to.

Because you've helped me so much, Henry. I don't know what would have become of me if you hadn't come into my life, if—" His voice caught in his throat, and he couldn't complete his thought.

"Hush," she soothed, leaning close to him as she gazed into his eyes. "I think we saved each other."

And then she pressed her lips to his, and he knew in his heart that he was truly home.

* * * * *

Dear Reader,

Thank you for allowing me to share Henry and Chandler's story. I've always liked the story of the prodigal son. The word *prodigal* describes a person who recklessly spends money, but a prodigal son is a person who leaves home for a prodigal life and returns repentant. We've come to use this term to mean any person who leaves a righteous life to lead a wayward one and returns remorseful. I cherish the idea that we can go astray and still find our way home to God and an honorable life. One of the lessons I was reminded of when reading Luke 15 in preparation for writing this book was the importance of always being willing to open our arms to welcome a man or woman back into the fold.

Now that Henry and Chandler have found a good and happy life, it's time for me to focus on the pretty Koffman sister Willa. Everyone in Honeycomb thought that Willa would be the first to marry, but she's struggling to find a man she can love. I'm hoping I can help her!

Blessings,
Emma Miller